Who

Couldn't Die

by Rick Gillis

First published in Canada in 2017 by Rick Gillis

ISBN: 9781542773553

I would like to dedicate this book to Jeanne, without whose unwavering support it would not have been possible.

ACKNOWLEDGMENTS

There are many who helped me in writing *The Boy Who Couldn't Die* but I want to express my most sincere thanks to my wonderful, supportive wife Jeanne, who tirelessly coaxed me on, helped and guided me in my writing and was always there to bounce ideas off of and put me back on task when I waivered. I would also like to thank Vaughan Coupland who did an incredible job of editing my early drafts thus saving me the embarrassment of appearing the complete illiterate. Finally, a thank you goes to my great friend, Darcy Logan, who provided an honest and constructive critique along the way.

"Everything you can imagine is real."
Pablo Picasso

PROLOGUE

"For fuck sake, grow up."

To be clear, I never actually heard my dad say this. He was a man who, despite his hair trigger temper, held his tongue around us kids. In fact, I actually never heard my dad use the term fuck in any of its forms until, at the age of about fourteen; I went to work for him for the summer. And though my pals and I had been using language like this--and pretty much all of its kin--from the tender age of eleven or so, I was shocked to hear it peel off the lips of my father.

Though his sentiments regarding me were never actually verbalized, I know that they formed visibly and crystal-clear in my dad's mind on more than one occasion, and more likely than not, in those exact words.

It isn't as if this sentiment existed in a vacuum. Although doubtlessly aware of much of our youthful misdeeds, it is most unlikely he could have known them all, the certainty of this being that I am here today telling this story.

Growing up in a small, tough, mountain coal-mining town, right in the middle of two very similar towns and two villages, whose youth did not let the size of their environs diminish their taste for trouble, made youthful devilment almost a way of life. Oh, for sure there were the quiet ones, but in our town you could count them on your fingers and have a few left over. Even some of the quiet boys merely used their deferential personas as specious camouflage. The vast majority constituted a profusion of youthful bad-assery, in varying degrees.

Were you fortunate enough to get through your pre-pubescent years unscathed, it most certainly would catch you up as you struggled through adolescence... altar boys to petty burglars, musical protégés to car thieves, teachers' pets to shoplifters, and on and on. Peer pressure trumped good sense every time. In small towns, unlike larger cities, there seemed few safe havens from the persistence of these pressures. Even an organization as noble in its aims as the Cub Scouts became little more than a catalyst for bad behavior unbecoming of the movement. Lord Baden Powell would have flipped over in his grave.

The 1950s and 60s were times markedly different from today. No, it wasn't the Norman Rockwell *"mom in the kitchen, apple pie cooling on the window sill era."* Close, for sure, but we had already gone a bit past that. We were, after all, the generation that had ushered in that upheaval decade of the 70s.

Looking back on it from the vantage point of advanced years, the question of why has stuck with me. *Why* was growing up in those years so markedly different from what it is today? It truly was, and by no small measure.

Perhaps it was about freedom.

It was a freedom not without a degree of responsibility. To suggest a lack of discipline in which we were permitted to run wild and unchecked would be a mischaracterization. No, there were nearly always consequences and discipline was doled out generously when our adults found it necessary. This meant, ultimately, that shit flew randomly.

We weren't raised solely by our parents but by an entire community of parents. Looking back now, I'm certain that I was chastised as often by the mother or father (or big brother) of a friend, as I was by my own folks. With rare exception, parents were okay with this arrangement.

Truth? There were a few fathers in our neighborhood that I was scared shitless of.

Parents rarely worried much when you went out the door, where you were going or what you would be up to. "Be home for supper," were my mother's predictable parting words, usually spoken over her shoulder from the kitchen as I streaked out the back door with or without my dog tagging behind me. That was about it. Response was implied.

So it was that we had this unspoken liberty. With such license came a veritable smorgasbord of misdeeds, some bordering on outright criminality, others just plain stupid, and still others potentially lethal. Fact is, not all of us made it to adulthood and those of us who did can claim at least one casualty in our circle of friends.

There was one, however. He was a close friend

to us all who, by all manner of probability, should have left us on any number of occasions. I'm going to tell you the story of Little Ricky Callaghan.

"Little Ricky" was the moniker he wore well into his late teens and one I'm sure he felt like kicking into the ditch on more than one occasion. By physical stature and the fact that he wore glasses, he fit the name. He was smaller than most of the other boys he hung with and carried the appearance of frailty. In a time when about one in ten boys wore eyeglasses, it was considered a sign of weakness. But in Ricky's case appearance was where it ended.

He was deceptively wiry and strong, and short of the occasional teasing from some of the older neighborhood boys, he really took no guff. The eyeglasses came off on more than one occasion and the long-term result of this was that he garnered a reputation as a pretty good scrapper and not one to be messed with lightly. He certainly didn't win them all, but he never backed down, and the ones he did lose always convinced his adversary not to go down that road again. To my knowledge, he was never in a fight twice with the same person.

If Little Ricky's appearance was misleading on

the fisticuffs front, it was equally true with regard to his penchant for mischief. He positively exuded innocence. But if there was something going on in the neighborhood or some other part of town that wasn't quite up to the benchmark of acceptable the probability was high that he and his ever-present circle of like-minded friends could be found right smack in the middle of it.

Oh yeah, and there was that ever present dog of his, Rusty. Ricky always insisted Rusty was a cocker spaniel, but his mixed lineage was given to question by his odd reddish color, set off with a white diamond-shaped patch between his eyes and an additional few touches of white on his front paws. It's not as though any boy would actually consider lionizing the merits of his dog based upon its pedigree. The fact of it was that there were no purebred dogs in the neighborhood and short of those few telltale white markings, Rusty came as close as any of them to representing any sort of canine purity whatsoever.

Not having spent a great deal of time—well, actually no time at all—on the study of human personality development, I'm ill-equipped to make any pronouncements whatsoever in this field. However, it hasn't escaped me that there are those who are viewed by others around them, throughout their entire lives, by one defining moment in that life. Human nature, after all, seeks to explain the why of things. It's not a stretch, then, to believe the corollary--that a single defining moment may well become the blueprint, so to speak, of how that person lives his life. Since this is not an academic treatise, however, I shall say no more on the matter and leave it to you to contemplate as we move on.

2.25 P.M. Thursday September 15, 1953
East R.R. Crossing Blairmore

On a warm fall afternoon five-year-old Ricky Cal-
laghan and his best pal, Kenny Zemancik, headed
downtown with their allowance money to buy comic
books. It was 1953, and his family, including mom,
dad and older siblings, had just moved to the
Crowsnest Pass the prior summer. His father, Ernest
Callaghan, better known as Ernie, had taken a rather
senior job as millwright and machinist at Rocky
Mountain Sawmills. His wife Elizabeth was a stay-
at-home mom, taking care of a blended family of kids
with Ricky being the youngest. The family had packed
up and moved to the Pass from Campbell River on
Vancouver Island. Among other reasons, the lumber
mills on the coast were just getting too big and too un-
ionized for Ernie's liking, and he and Elizabeth were
welcoming the chance to make a new start with their
blended family in a much smaller and more intimate

community. Ernie had some sought-after skills that included millwright certification and mid-level management experience. The position offered at Rocky Mountain Sawmills seemed tailor made for him.

Like so many western communities, Blairmore was one of those typical mountain towns that grew up around the Canadian Pacific Railroad as it forged its link across the country and up through the high passes of the Rockies. What made the Crowsnest Pass different from many of the others, however, was that the CPR had an appetite for coal, and the Pass sat on one of the richest deposits of high-grade coal in the country. By the time the Callaghan family arrived, the whole area was awash in prosperity and the lumber industry was booming right along with it.

The Callaghan family purchased a large, two-story home two blocks south of the railway tracks. Within a few months everyone in the family got used to the noise from the freight trains as they rumbled through the town several times a day, blasting their horns at every one of the town's four crossings.

Blairmore's main street ran parallel to and just 50 yards north of the CPR tracks. It was the town's main street, but it did double duty as Highway 3; one of only three major routes through the Rocky Mountains *straddling Alberta and British Columbia. Though significantly less travelled than the TransCanada Highway to the north, it was a major well-travelled artery. This seemingly inconsequential bit of geographical information is important to this story as it unfolds.*

Ricky didn't remember his mother's warnings about the dangers of the railway tracks, but that didn't mean that she hadn't done so. After all, it was pretty much one of those things that every parent just automatically did if you lived that close to such an obvious danger, kind of like, "now remember to brush your teeth after dinner, and, oh yeah, stay away from the tracks".

Furthermore, it was doubtful the two adventuring five-year-olds had any sort of parental permission to set off downtown by themselves in the first place. For the sake of those readers who harbor a contemporary sense of parental responsibility, let's assume there was no such permission, for the purpose here is not to discredit the parenting practices of 1950s rural Canada but to set the stage for what was about to happen.

It was only two blocks, but one can imagine the excitement shared by the two pals on their first solo venture downtown. When they reached the railway crossing Kenny went over the tracks and continued on. In his excitement he was oblivious to the fact that his buddy was no longer at his side. No, being the inquisitive child that he was, Ricky had stopped in the middle of the crossing and was gazing in rapt intrigue up the length of the tracks, particularly to where they went over a short trestle that bridged Lyons Creek. Curiosity aroused, he walked a few steps toward the trestle to take a little closer look at it and the creek that it spanned. Fully captivated by his new surroundings he didn't think for a second to look over his shoulder.

He gave little thought to that faint rumble under his feet since it meant nothing to him. The first, and only, warning of the westbound train's approach was the loud and piercing blare of its horn. Ricky had heard the horn dozens of times before but from his home two blocks away. Startled, he turned to see the massive front of the engine bearing down on him. He froze. Seized with terror he could only watch as the train approached at full speed. The repeated panicked blaring of its horn only added to the fear that kept him glued to the middle of the track.

Fifty yards away, and startled by the frequency of the train's horn, a Highways Department bridge construction crew was working on replacing a highway

bridge over the same Lyons Creek. Alerted by the un-
usual frenzy of noise from the train, they all looked on
in horror at the certain tragedy unfolding before their
eyes. They stood, as frozen as the child on the track,
paralyzed with terror as the train bore down on the
helpless five-year-old.

All of them, that is, but one.

Nineteen-year-old Brenden McLeish was the
youngest of the large crew working on the bridge that
day. Like his crewmates, he too was transfixed by
what was playing out as he stared at the helpless child-
-but for no longer than a split second. Nobody knows
why, perhaps not even the young McLeish himself, but
he sprang to action.

In a full sprint through the mostly dried-up creek
bed and up the steep embankment on its other side he
reached the petrified child seconds ahead of the train.
"He was crying, had his hands over his eyes and I
heard him say, 'It's going to run over me,'" McLeish
recounted in a newspaper article lauding his incredi-
ble bravery.

Tackling Ricky in a desperate dive across the
track, the two bodies landed hard but safely out of the
path of certain death. "We didn't move, not an inch,"
said McLeish "I was on top of him and his head was
resting on the end of the rail tie and he was looking

12

straight up as the wheels went by. I knew I was crushing him with my weight, but I just couldn't risk moving, even slightly. We stayed like that for some time, even after the train had passed. I could hear the piercing squeal of metal on metal as the engineer was bringing the train to an emergency stop. The rest of my crew got there by then and helped us back on our feet. I looked down the track and could see the back of the caboose nearly a hundred yards away. The train had finally stopped and I could see one of the guys from the caboose running back down the track towards us. The little guy was still crying and trembling like a leaf."

Ricky was so traumatized by what had just happened that his mind went blank for those hours following his near death. The memory of that time had been erased from his mind completely, never to return. The bridge crew, en masse, had walked him, still-shaking and crying, back to his house with directions provided by a few of the neighbors who had arrived late to the scene. His friend Kenny tagged behind the group he, too, in shock from what had nearly happened to his friend.

At home, not a word was ever spoken of it again. Ever.

The child, snatched at the last minute from certain

death, never got a chance until many years later to personally thank his rescuer for his bravery. For years to come he would be awakened in the middle of the night with the memory of lying face up, head pressed to the end of the wooden railway tie with its smell of creosote, a large heavy man who lay protectively on top of him, and the steel wheels of the train, inches from his head, clacking by seemingly endlessly.

His mother would put him back to sleep with a gentle hug, soft words and sometimes a small glass of warm milk. She would dry her own tears and slip back into her bed.

A SISTER'S JOURNAL
Kathryn Callaghan

Chapter 1

Stumbling Out of the Gate

There was something different about my brother Ricky; something that I was never quite able to put my finger on. He simply wasn't like the other boys. It just may have been because I was his older sister, and close enough in age to feel a deep and warmly satisfying closeness with him. Don't get me wrong; typically, we did have our fair share of spats, in spite of, or perhaps because of, my sisterly over-protectiveness. I was only slightly older than he but had always been infinitely more mature.

I always felt that something had affected him as a result of the train incident. He had changed after that taking risks with seemingly little regard for his own safety, or for that matter, the safety of the friends around him. I don't know. I can just tell you how I felt. Our closeness may have come from the fact that he was my only true, full sibling in a blended family of kids: two each from my mom's and dad's previous marriages, then Ricky and me born just about two years apart.

The big age difference was between Ricky and me and our three older brothers and one older sister. By the time my brother and I had hit our adolescent years the older ones had all gone off and had left home for good. My brother and I used to joke with each other that we were the only true Callaghans anyway, and the other four were just half breeds.

It may have been just a joke, but in reality there was this crystal clearness in the relationship that we shared. By comparison, it seemed that an indefinable, translucent haze hung over everything else in my life extending to our parents, older siblings and even our circles of friends. It was always puzzling to me, and on those occasions when my brain seemed compelled to confront it, it was more than a little disquieting. More than once I was tempted to ask my brother if he experienced these same feelings, but feared he would just laugh it off as he was prone to do when I became too morose.

I couldn't help but feel that much of it was somehow connected to the dream. That dream, changing only slightly each time, shared my sleep more often than I cared it to. It wasn't unpleasant; not a nightmare. In fact, it embodied in its unworldliness a peaceful serenity. Part of me wanted it gone, while the rest was content to languish in its euphoria.

Each time, Ricky and I would descend hand in hand down a gentle path into a lush and wonderful narrow valley. The spectacular colors of nature were all around us, from the green vinery that trailed down the steep canyon walls to trees and shrubbery festooned with blossoms of every imaginable color. They, and the soft grasses and flowers, were fed by a ribbon-like, tall, thin waterfall at the far end of the canyon which turned into dozens of tiny rivulets and small, deep pools of cool water.

Then there were the animals: tigers and wolves, small prides of lions, and large, multicolored snakes that hung from the trees while others slithered through the tall grasses. Reptilian creatures would crawl out from some of the deep pools to sun themselves on flat black basalt stones, seemingly placed there for that very purpose. Hawks, eagles and other smaller birds would duck in and out of the valley or perch themselves on the tree branches to survey the paradise below them.

In this Eden of tranquility, we were the only

people.

As we strolled past the animals, particularly the reptiles and cats, I would feel my brother's small hand tighten on mine. I'd squeeze his back and say, "Don't be afraid, Ricky, they can't see us." I had been here before.

Once, I tried to describe my recurring dream to Ricky and it turned out to be a losing effort. I had to listen to his stories, but he didn't feel equally inclined to take my dream account very seriously.

"That place in your dream sounds almost like that awful Yosemite Park oil painting mom and dad have hanging on the living room wall."

"Kind of," I thought, temporarily surprised that he'd absorbed any of my story at all.

"Katty, maybe that's why you don't smile or laugh enough," he said to me, showing a bit more sensitivity than I gave him credit for.

Katty. He'd given me that name from the time he spoke his first baby words and couldn't quite manage the "th" sound. It had stuck. Those few times when he referred to me as Kathryn provided a pretty good hint that he was upset with me for one reason or another.

When I gave further thought to what he said, though, it dawned on me that he might have been right. My dream world was beautiful and safe. Reality felt hard and perplexing.

My brother was never one for any sort of serious introspection, or so I thought. He seemed to live life skipping across its surface and experiencing the thrills of doing rather than the deeper satisfaction I sought from frequent self-scrutiny. My staid personality also disguised a keen sense of observation, so I took in more of what was around me than people might have thought and my memory was as keen and sharp as a butcher's blade.

Oh, the joys of introversion.

Yes, I was the quiet one--unadventurous, pliant and frankly, a little bit bookish and boring. My friends were few but close. They were generally girls just like myself who shared that unenviable place in the social strata just outside that ever-present circle of popularity. At least I wasn't alone there. The one exception to that was my very closest friend, Marlene Arsene, who I always referred to as my alter ego but most certainly not my muse. I don't know if she really understood the full implications of what that meant, but she knew for certain that she occupied a very special place in my life, and I in hers.

Marlene was pretty with beautiful dark shiny hair that came down almost to her waist. You would have thought that a girl with her obvious physical attributes, those classic Spanish features, would carry herself with some degree of decorum. In truth, she was shallow and flighty. If she were to ever find herself carrying two thoughts at one time she'd have to set one down. The boys loved her though, and she them. By the time I'd gone out on my first date, well into my teens I might add, she'd worked her way through nearly half the boys at school.

We were an unlikely friendship, me with my mouse brown hair, unremarkable features and boy- ish body. Marlene was out of her training bra and into a 34B before she turned fourteen. I was still stuffing mine with Kleenex. We Callaghans were, in a word, plain.

Ricky, as virtually everyone called him, never got a really great start in life, a situation that had a great and lasting effect on him as he grew up. Born with one wandering eye as they called it then, he required critical corrective surgery at a very tender age. The surgery was new at the time and the success rates, my parents were told, were one in ten. Ricky was one of the lucky ones. Though successful in straightening out his eye and saving him the stigma of being labeled cross-eyed, it left him with poor vision requiring him to wear glasses from then on to his perpetual dismay.

After the surgery he had to wear that eye patch over his good eye for months in an effort to strengthen the bad one, all with limited success. In his typical upbeat manner, he took it well though, and during that time likened himself to a pirate. I found myself on the receiving end of a few whacks on my backside with the flat side of his sword, fashioned hastily from a piece of old lath he found laying out in the alley behind our place.

To our mother's frustration, he had the annoying habit of removing his glasses by gripping the temples on either side like he was gripping a baseball bat and yanking them off in the most indelicate way. Mom refused to buy him the more fashionable plastic frames until he changed his ways. In some respects, my brother was a slow learner. As a result, he wore the more resilient wire-rimmed glasses until he was almost ten. They were decidedly uncool and my poor brother bore the brunt of ongoing ridicule, not so much from the kids his age but by the older ones in the neighborhood and at school.

Those wire-rimmed glasses hung off his face, perpetually twisted, bent and crooked, with finger and thumbprints all over the lenses, forcing Ricky to crane his neck forward to see, like he was trying to peer through a frosted window. The posture that this created made him look even geekier.

"I don't know how you can even see through those things," I'd tell him often. "With all those greasy fingerprints all over them those lenses look like that wax paper mom wraps our sandwiches in."

Finally, it became nearly impossible to buy the wire-rimmed glasses. Due to their obvious unpopularity getting them required a special order. Mom relented, but only after the requisite round of threats. Ricky became one of the best customers Dr. Bishop, our local optometrist, had with repairs required to his new plastic-rimmed glasses at least once a month. Dr. Bishop would straighten everything out, replace whatever needed replacing, clean the finger smudged lenses with a soft cloth and vinegar solution, then place them gently back on my brother's face.

Every visit would end with the same caution,

"If you don't take better care of those lenses, son, you're going to go totally blind." That warning had about as much effect on Ricky as telling him his teeth would fall out if he didn't stop eating candy.

In spite of all the teasing over his vision, and the misfortune of also having a youthful immune system that was so weak that he caught almost everything that came along from chicken pox to mumps, my brother was the most cheerful boy I had ever known. He shone a light into some of the darker corners of my own personality; me, the one who seldom was sick and was the very picture of good health, despite my plainness. He never failed to raise my spirits. Often it was just the little things. I would catch him from time to time, all alone, singing or humming some catchy little childish ditty quietly to himself, and I would slip away unnoticed with a smile lit up across my face. He filled me with joy and he didn't even know it.

It was that indomitable spirit that made my brother the dynamic little guy that he was and yet there always seemed to be something absent; some peculiar, gnawing darkness around the very edge of my life that left me with an unsettling feeling in the very core of me. It was an inexplicable stirring, removed somewhat from actual dread, and balanced with an equal measure of intermittent anxiety. It wasn't there before. Not before the train.

With no plausible explanation, I chalked it all up to my solicitous nature and the onset of a more mature and sentient self. I longed though, for the unencumbered love I had for him before that September day in 1953. Try as I might to ignore it, the strange uneasiness persisted. After some time, it just became a part of me, a melancholic cast over an otherwise joyful youth. It came and went like a rainy day. No one really took notice of it. I was a quiet girl.

Chapter 2

The Angel and the Rascal

Yes, the quiet one, the good one, as I was told on more than one occasion. That may have been couched in relative terms, however, since my "little brother," as my girlfriends called him, certainly could never have been branded as that. It was true, though. I spoke little, was studious and serious, was seldom in trouble at home and never so at school. Ricky often bore the brunt of scholastic comparison from his teachers, many of whom only a few years earlier had had the pleasure of schooling an honors student such as myself.

"Mrs. Cruikshank doesn't think you and I are real brother and sister," he said to me one day. Mrs. Cruikshank was the Grade Two teacher at Central School. She was a tough old bird who rewarded A students, like myself, while bringing down the wrath of Hades on those not so academically fortunate. She was the bane of existence for my

26

brother and, due to his stubborn nature, it was re-ciprocated.

"Oh, and why does she think that?" I asked cautiously, sensing the insincerity in his indignation.

"Maybe it's because you're the brain and I'm the dunce," he replied. "She really doesn't like me. This is the tenth time this year that she's given me the strap. Every time she has, she's told me that she wishes I were more like you. I've had more strappings from her than any other kid in my class."

"Now, you're just feeling sorry for yourself," I said. "I'm sure she didn't strap you for being stupid, or maybe she did. What did you do this time?"

"She caught me climbing in through the open classroom window after recess this afternoon. How does that earn a strapping? Johnny Powell was the one who boosted me up so I could get in and he never got it."

"Well, Johnny didn't get caught red-handed, did he?" I replied.

"I just want you to know that it's not that easy being your little brother," he shot back at me, abruptly ending the conversation. I had to choke back from laughing at the thought of the shoe being on the other foot. Love him as I did, I had always thought him to be the thorn in my side, not vice versa.

Nevertheless, I had the overwhelming urge to get the last word in on this one.

"Well," I said, "I'm sorry that I'm the one responsible for you getting all those strappings. Since Mrs. Cruikshank likes me so much, maybe I'll have a little chat with her and ask her to lighten up on you a bit." I'm not sure that Ricky was old enough to understand sarcasm because he gave me a little smile. I always hated it when I wasted perfectly good mockery on him.

Though I was not the classic loner I gathered around me, with few exceptions, friends who shared my disdain for the frivolous, flighty and fashionable. I preferred instead those who were there, by my hand, to make my social life solid and secure.

I didn't need all the hoopla, disingenuous drama and mendacity that went along with being part of the school's inner circle. I had Ricky. And by a different measure, Ricky had me. Although lacking in the visceral pleasures of real experience, a life of derivative delight suited me just fine. It was served up to me almost daily in the quietly spoken transgressions entrusted to me in the attic bedrooms my brother and I shared for most of our growing up years.

We would sit there for long periods of time, either in his bedroom or mine, as he poured out his day from as mundane an event as failing an arithmetic test, to vandalism over at the old West Canadian Mine tipple. It was true, all of it, its veracity more often than not supported by others or general community gossip. I felt as though in a great adventure story: a participant who bore neither concern nor responsibility for outcome, or so I thought... for the first little while, anyway. Then I slowly began to take on the trappings of a genuine accomplice; a position I neither invited nor truly relished.

There was one thing you could be nearly certain of. If there was mischief going on in the neighborhood, my brother was a part of it or at least was privy to it. Whether his devil-may-care attraction to trouble was the result of his near brush with death or not, I never gave thought to question. At least not until much later, when things began stacking up and I could view them in retrospect.

To be sure, he did not suffer extreme discipline at home. He occupied a soft spot in our mother's heart, for good reason I was to discover. And our father, a man of quick temperament, had very early backed away from physically disciplining him, also for good reason.

"When was the last time mom gave you a really good tanning?" I asked him one day after he'd received only a stern scolding when she caught him booting the neighbour's cat.

He had to mull over that one for a moment. "I think it was that time I was over playing at Francine's place and didn't come home for supper," he said.

"That was two years ago," I bawled, frustration obvious in my tone. "You should have got it good for kicking old man Vyrsholik's cat last week, especially when mom caught you red handed doing it."

"It was digging and crapping in her pea patch again," Ricky replied in defense.

"Yeah, well mom shoos him out of the garden when he's in there. She doesn't punt him over the fence."

"I didn't kick him over the fence. He jumped

30

over after I kicked him."

This conversation was going absolutely no-where.

After a time, I came to understand that this was simply my cross to bear. I realized I wasn't the good girl in order to avoid punishment and my brother wasn't the bad boy to invite it. We were who we were.

Before this epiphany it was occasionally my practice to whine in a sniveling sort of way, over the fact that my baby brother was spoiled and that both mom and dad favored him over me, and, to some small measure, there may have been some truth to that. In all fairness, however, dad had always babied the girls in his life equally and was somewhat less lenient toward the boys.

"You should quit feeling so damn sorry for yourself all the time," my older half-sister, Paula, barked to me one day as I was attempting to use her as a sounding board for my self-pity. Paula could be very blunt with me sometimes. "Yes, mom does have a soft spot in her heart for Ricky. What you don't know is why. Mom suffered mild epilepsy for much of her life," she continued.

"Even before you came along she was having seizures. I remember one really bad one she had when I was little, right on the kitchen floor. It was terrifying. When Ricky was born, for some unknown reason, her seizures stopped and never returned. In her heart she connected that to all the health problems Ricky had as a baby. Mom truly believes he exorcised her sickness. That won't ever change, so stop your bellyaching."

So there it was. I finally understood. It was an unspoken bond even greater than one normally held by a mother for her child. The funny part was that Ricky had no clue of this at all. And I would never tell him.

As for dad, his frequent temper outbursts were famous in our small community. Everyone had a favorite "Ernie Callaghan blow up" anecdote, and unfortunately it came to be what defined him— publicly, that is.

Though as kids we'd all experienced his violent explosions, we also knew that underneath all that bluster was a soft and caring father and husband. He was never physical with either Ricky or myself, but a tongue-lashing from him was far worse than any corporal punishment mom could hand out even with the dreaded wooden spoon.

As for me, I worried little, seldom deserving any form of punishment at all. The few times Ricky was punished it was always by our mother, and I wondered about that. One afternoon it, too, was explained to me, again by Paula, as we were doing the supper dishes together.

"Ricky doesn't get that many lickings," I casually mentioned to her, careful this time not to sound too whiny. "And when he does it's always mom who gives them. Come to think of it, dad never does give out lickings."

"Oh, there's good reason for that," Paula replied. "He used to give us older ones some pretty good ones with a big leather straight razor strop, but he stopped."

"Why?" I asked.

Paula gazed, without expression, out the kitchen window as she recalled. "Ricky was really young, actually it was even before the train incident. For some reason he'd stuck some copper wire he found on dad's workbench into the power plug-in out in the laundry room and blew out a whole bunch of fuses. You know him. He does these dumb things sometimes. Dad just lost it. After he replaced the fuses and had the power back on he took Ricky to the bathroom, put him over his knee and gave him five or six good whacks with the strop."

"Strop? What's a strop?" I interrupted.

"Dad used to shave with a straight razor," Paula explained, a little impatient with me for breaking up her train of thought. "Strops were big, wide leather straps that were used to sharpen straight razors. Dad had stopped using a straight razor years ago, but hung onto the strop for—uh, shall I say--disciplinary purposes. Anyway," she continued, "when it was done, dad stomped out of the bathroom, still in a huff and slammed the door behind him. Ricky let out a scream like I'd never heard before and dad thought he was throwing a tantrum. He turned around and began giving him another spanking right there on the spot. Then mom noticed a big red welt on Ricky's arm and re-alized that the scream was because he'd caught it in the door when dad had slammed it. Mom yelled at him to stop, but he didn't. She had to step in and pull Ricky away, yelling at dad at the same time. It was all really crazy. Then mom pointed to the mark on Ricky's arm that dad hadn't noticed. I never saw him like that before," Paula went on, "I thought he was actually going to cry and it seemed as though he just got smaller, physically, I mean. I can't explain it. He walked over to the garbage can under the sink and threw the strop away. He never laid a hand on any of us again, and as you probably know by now, the job became mom's."

"Where was I when all this happened?" I asked. "I don't remember any of it, except that I seem to recall Ricky having a pretty big bruise on his arm."

"I don't know," said Paula. "You were probably outside playing or something."

Chapter 3

A Guided Missile

Today mom and dad were called to the hospital. Ricky was there. Unconscious. It was absolute pandemonium around the house until dad got home from work to pick mom up and drive to the hospital. Mom was crying and dad had to hold her briefly and get her calmed down before they got in the truck.

They asked Peggy, the next door neighbor, if she could look after me while they were gone. School was out for the summer holidays. I was the only one home at the time and not quite old enough to take care of myself.

"What happened to Ricky?" I asked, certain that I wasn't going to get any sort of clear answer. I was scared for my brother, but in their obvious panic, mom and dad didn't seem to understand nor even acknowledge my concern. As I grew older I would learn to live with the exclusion I felt each time something traumatic happened in the family. I chalked it up to protectiveness on the part of my parents, but I could never escape the feeling that there was something more to it than that.

"I want to come with you," I pleaded to no avail. Peggy took me gently by the hand and we went to her house. She poured me a big glass of orange Kool-Aid and let me sit outside on the back step with her orange cat, Ginger.

When they got to the hospital Ricky was just coming to and already had a pretty big goose egg on the top of his noggin. No broken bones, no blood, and no signs of concussion. My brother had dodged another one. At this point I still had absolutely no idea what that was.

They all got home about mid-afternoon, Ricky went straight up to his room. Dad went back to work and mom never spoke a word, other than to tell me Ricky was all right and to ask, "Did you get lunch?"

She sent me out to play, explaining only that my brother needed his rest, and that was that. Supper that evening would have been the pride of a Buddhist monastery; the conversation decidedly brief and evasive. It always seemed that when something serious happened in our family there was little or no discussion of it. Everyone just clammed up. Even the older ones kept their comments to themselves. That night was no exception. I never understood that.

Ricky spent dinner pushing his food around on his plate and saying nothing at all. It was a noted departure from his usual chatty self. I was dying to know what the heck had happened, but I knew I would have to wait for later when we were alone together. That seemed desperately far off.

"What happened?" I asked, almost the moment we were finally alone upstairs. We were bedding down for the night and it was the first time Ricky and I had actually even talked to one another all that day. I was sitting on the edge of his bed and he was propped up against a pillow in the corner idly re-reading one of his Superman comic books.

"I don't really know," he said, "other than what I overheard at the hospital after I came to. One thing I do know is that mom and dad were too upset to even give me heck. Donna's bike is wrecked and I guess I'm just lucky to be here. That's what mom said, anyway... about fifteen times."

"But, what happened?" I repeated in frustration. "No one will talk to me."

"I'll tell you what I remember," he said, "But it isn't much."

"It'll probably be a lot more than anyone else around here has told me," I said.

"Well," Ricky started, "You know my friend Nick's dad got him his first bike at the end of the school year as a reward for passing and he's let me try riding it a few times. I was getting pretty good at it, too."

"Whoa, whoa," I interrupted. "I don't need you to go that far back."

"Okay," he continued, "this morning I was looking at all the bikes we have in our shed and realized that since Paula's is a girl's bike and doesn't have a bar, I could probably ride it. So, I decided to give it a try. I wheeled it out into the alley and even though it was way too big for me, I could actually peddle it because there was no bar in the way. I got going down the alley pretty fast and came out onto the street. I could see Mr. Tinordi coming up the street in that old green Plymouth of his and I just panicked. I think it would have been too late to put the brakes on, anyway. The last thing I remember is just hitting the side of his car and going over the handlebars. That was all."

"You could have been killed," I hissed at him, slapping him girlishly on the hand.

"Yeah, mom told me that, too."

"So that's all you know?" I went on.

"I overheard mom and dad talking with Mr. Tinordi at the hospital. He was really shook up and was apologizing to them like crazy, as though it was his fault or something. He told dad that when the bike hit the side of his car I actually flew over the top of the handlebars and went right through his open passenger side window. Then I banged my head on the armrest on his side of the car and it knocked me out. He told dad that I was unconscious, lying right on his lap and he didn't even stop the car. He just drove straight to the hospital. I don't really remember any of it. I don't even remember going through Mr. Tinordi's window. I must have had my eyes closed by then."

"Oh, Ricky, when are you going to learn?" I was in tears now. "First the train, now this. You've scared mom and dad half to death. I don't think you'll be getting a bike of your own any time soon."

"Oh, sure I will," he replied, overly cocky now. "Dad wouldn't want me breaking up any more bikes that aren't mine."

The one thing about my brother that annoyed me the most was his cheekiness after a close call like this one. Seven-year-olds aren't supposed to be such big shots, but he took a good crack at it.

"Wanna feel the goose egg?" he asked, rubbing the top of his head gently.

I didn't give him the benefit.

Chapter 4

The Copper Pimple

Ricky and I lived with an unspoken agreement. Why it came to be that I don't really know. He was able to share confidences with me that he probably couldn't share with anyone else. Sometimes, I know he needed to brag, just a little bit. In all that time we seldom spoke our feelings, like our world was made up solely of events and happenings, and nothing more. Being more the introvert and functioning on a significantly more emotional level, I always found this a little troubling. Questioning it was useless. Ricky could never connect with such a concern.

My brother spoke to a need in me and any attempt by myself to broaden the scope of it could make it all go away. I feared such a loss.

There were times along the way when I had to take that uncomfortable accomplice role, however.

Then there were other instances when the duality of my position as trusted confidante and dutiful daughter resulted in moral crises.

Now, when I look back, I don't regret the lies I told mom and dad in order to protect Ricky. If it were that important to them I rationalized, they would certainly make the effort to divine the truth by other means. The eyes and ears of our little community were everywhere, after all, and secrets were difficult to cover up.

Ricky figured that one out early, too, so his "work around" was never to deny the event itself, or its results, but to garnish the details so generously that it mitigated his wrongdoing.

Outcomes could seldom be denied, but the events leading to them certainly could. My brother was a lovable little rogue, but he was no fool, and very early in life he understood the philosophy of plausible deniability. "Remember, Katty," he confided to me one day, "never tell a lie that doesn't contain at least a grain of truth."

That was almost too clever for a boy of his tender years. Good advice is good advice no matter the source. I rarely had to use it myself, but there were more than a few occasions when I had to stand quietly by while Ricky put it into practical application.

Both mom and dad were dead set against firearms of any sort, which may have been fine had they decided to stay out on the west coast in their urban watery surroundings. But here we were in the mountains. The woods around town--always referred to as the bush—teemed with squirrels, rabbits, chipmunks, tin cans, beer bottles and other targets: a paradise of stuff to shoot at for any kid with a gun.

Denying your boy a firearm was tantamount to living on the coast and not letting him have a fishing rod. There was hardly a boy in our neighborhood that didn't have a pocket or hunting knife by the time he was seven, a BB or pellet gun at nine or ten, and a .22 rifle before he was thirteen. My brother was one of the exceptions with respect to the .22 at least. The flaw in our parents' logic was simply that every one of Ricky's friends owned a .22 and as a result all that my brother had to do was provide his own ammo.

So it was that I became complicit in one of Ricky's first "biggy" lies. Fortunately for him it pre-dated the .22 rifle years or this journal would have come to an end prematurely.

It's difficult to come home with blood streaming down your face from a hole in your forehead
and not have a pretty good yarn as to the how of
it. The gist of it was that he and his pals were just
throwing stones down by the river when a chip
from one of the rocks flew up and hit him in the
forehead right between his eyes. Ricky embellished
the story with so much needless detail that the be-
lievability scale went from about a two to a nine.
After some doctoring and a minor scolding from
our mom on the dangers of throwing rocks, the
whole incident seemed forgotten. Call it sisterly in-
tuition or whatever, I just knew there was much,
much more to it than that. I could hardly wait until we were alone to ferret out the truth, which I
was certain he would share with me.

"OK, so tell me what really happened today?"
I demanded. I couldn't resist smiling at the huge
gob of gauze and tape mom had put on his forehead
with the instruction that he wasn't to remove it
until she said so. Mom had wisdom and good instincts so it didn't escape me that this might possibly have been her little response to my brother's
plausible deniability. A little embarrassment never
hurt anyone.

The real story required very little prodding on

my part, almost as though Ricky was relieved to finally unload the truth.

"We were all playing down by the river, all right, but the game was cowboys and Indians," he began. "I was chasing Nick down the edge of the river yelling that I was going to scalp him. When I got close, he turned around and pointed his BB gun right at me and told me not to come any closer or he would shoot. Then the gun just went off accidentally and I could feel the BB hit me in the head."

I couldn't help it. My hands went up and grabbed both of my cheeks and I gasped in disbelief. "He shot you? Nick actually shot you?"

"It was an accident," Ricky repeated. "He didn't deliberately shoot me."

I believed that. Nick Costa was probably my brother's second best friend, and nearly a match for his misbehavior. They were pals but in that competitive way so typical of boys their age. The big difference in the two was that Ricky would make up excuses for his misdeeds. Nick was totally unapologetic. That was one of the reasons he was not one of my favorites. The little girlies liked him though, with his dark, Mediterranean good looks, athletic build and bad boy attitude--even Marlene, who frequently referred to him as "that cute little Wop."

My brother went on, "There was no blood right away, but when I felt my forehead I could feel where the hole was, and the BB was still there, under my skin and about a half inch from the hole. We knew I couldn't go home with the BB still stuck in my head," he added, looking at me as though I should be showing more appreciation for his outstanding judgment.

With the BB still under the skin, all five of the friends came to the conclusion that some form of the actual truth might, unfortunately, be necessary. That, it seemed, or some sort of field surgery.

Who really knows how boys think; certainly not me. But, herein is the logic as explained in detail to me by Ricky. "If our parents found out that there was actually a gun involved I would never own one for as long as I lived. Worse yet, the word would certainly get around and every one of my friends wouldn't, either. A few of them are very close to being allowed to have a .22. We had no choice," Ricky explained to me, a look of complete rational belief in his eyes, what little of them I could see under the huge bandage. "Between Nick,

Matt and I we squeezed the BB back to the hole and it popped right out. Then the blood really started to gush and I had to take off my sock and hold it over the hole to stop the bleeding."

I wriggled squeamishly on the edge of the bed as I visualized the whole thing.

As all this was happening none of the boys appear to have lost sight of the real reason for the on-site, self-administered first aid. It was simple logic. The BB had been successfully removed. Heads together, all of them were crafting the new, believable story and had agreed that, with the exception of Ricky, none of them would repeat it to their parents unless it became absolutely necessary.

I sat there dumbfounded and temporarily speechless. Finally, the only words that came out of me were, "You used your dirty, stinky sock?"

Telling him that he could have easily lost an eye was pointless since mom had already used that one up three or four times as she was bandaging up his forehead.

Oh, and one more thing... most of those boys did get their .22s. But not Ricky! He got a pellet gun, and that was a huge concession on our dad's part. That's another story for a little later chapter in his life.

The BB scar, as it turns out, was a foretelling. By the time my brother turned fourteen he'd added several others. He was quite the little mess. A rough inventory included the BB scar, a gash in his left eyebrow from having a jam can kicked squarely into his face, a diamond shaped scar on his upper cheekbone from a hockey stick, and a discolored front tooth from a tobogganing accident. Moving down, he had three self-inflicted knife wounds to his left hand and one to his right, the latter so nasty that our mother actually threw up tending to it. Then there was the deceptively small one on the front of his right foot, the result of him stabbing a ski pole completely through it.

Chapter 5

Never Ignore a Dog's Instincts

It's hard to talk about my brother without dedicating some of the conversation to Rusty.

Rusty was Ricky's dog, just in case you were wondering. When I say Ricky's dog it is with great emphasis, because in that dog's world there really was no one else. Let me say here that I fed him almost twice as often as my brother did, and it was me who played fetch with him in the back yard when Ricky didn't take him along. But that didn't matter. He was never going to be my dog.

I don't think there has been nearly enough study done on the relationship between young boys and their dogs. Who can really explain blind obedience with nary a word of discipline? Rusty would go to the ends of the earth for Ricky, and just for fun, my brother would often test that out, being the little shit that he was.

You couldn't call it cruelty. Ricky was never that. I would describe it more as benign neglect mixed in generously with a mutual need for companionship. After all, what dog could possibly enjoy being tossed into the icy water of the river off a fifteen-foot high bridge or run full out for miles while Ricky and his pals leisurely peddled their bikes at a speed about one mile an hour faster that the poor dog could run? In a nutshell, my brother and his little cocker spaniel (I use that description interchangeably with mutt) were simply inseparable and, in spite of what might have appeared to be one-sided affection, it was love.

That love affair seemed to have started from day one. Rusty had come into our family quite by accident. We were taking one of our weekend family car rides over to B.C. on a summer afternoon. It wasn't the nicest of days, as I recall. It had rained a bit. As we rounded a corner on the highway we could see something running toward us on the other side of the road, about a half a mile ahead. Dad pulled over and stopped the car and as it got closer we realized it was a dog.

Everyone just sat there looking but not Ricky. As the dog approached the car he opened the back door on his side and the little pooch veered across the road and just jumped right in; dirty, stinky, paws covered in mud and panting with the most revolting dog breath imaginable. He was all over my brother, wiggling wildly, and his little docked tail wagging uncontrollably. And he was licking my brother's face to everyone's disgust. I'd already squeezed myself as far as possible to the far side of the back seat in hopes of avoiding any of the unexpected affection.

"Eww," I cringed, "he stinks".

Our guest was past being a puppy, but he wasn't very old, either. Under the muck you could see that he had a beautiful, russet coat. But "he", as we discovered quickly as he rolled around on the seat, back legs spread wide, had no identifying collar or tags

"Well, he belongs to somebody," our dad finally said. "He's obviously lost and we can't just put him back out on the road. We'll have to see if we can find the owners."

The problem was we were miles away from the nearest town.

We spent the rest of the afternoon driving up and down the highway, checking out the few possible campgrounds and turnouts. Unfortunately for the dog, we found no one to claim him. Unfortunately for mom and dad, the afternoon also provided the time for my brother and Rusty, as he'd already named him, to bond. He barely got off his lap, and though the whole car reeked of wet dog, Ricky was oblivious to it.

What else could we do? We took Rusty home. Dad made what we all knew was a less than earnest effort to find the owners; a small classified ad in the local paper that appeared just once a week and a half later. In the meantime, Rusty had been all cleaned up and had settled comfortably into his new home with his new best friend. He was sweet and quite handsome, if I do say so myself. He'd also been trained, which was an added bonus.

"If we're going to keep him, you're going to have to feed him, give him water and take care of him," our mom admonished my brother when we knew for sure he was going to stay with us. That, as it turned out, was to be more of an admission that Rusty was Ricky's than it was a serious assignment of responsibility.

He became a part of the Callaghan family—for the next ten years.

"Did you know that Rusty saved my life today?" Ricky said to me one evening as we lolled around upstairs. Slightly distracted and thinking that this might be another of his lame stories, I just mumbled as I grabbed my new Nancy Drew mystery from the bookshelf.

"Nick, Matt and I were hiking up Cougar Mountain today," he went on seemingly oblivious to my disinterest. "We came to this weird patch of snow on the ground that was left over from winter. I was going to walk right across it and make a few snowballs to throw at the other guys. Before I could, Rusty just ran out in front of us, right across the snow. About half way across his hind legs went right through it. He managed to claw his way out with his front paws."

My brother had my interest now, and he knew it. He paused for a bit waiting for my prod that he knew was coming. His storytelling often bore the ear-markings of a really good public speaker, the guy who makes those timely pauses to allow for applause.

"That's it? That's the story? Rusty fell in a hole?" I said, knowing there was more, but also realizing that Ricky sought my undivided attention. I put Nancy Drew aside, to his satisfaction.

"There was this big, dark hole left in the middle of the patch," he went on, "and when we threw a few rocks down it you could hear them hitting off the sides for more than a few seconds. Then we could hear them splash. This thing must have been a few hundred feet deep. We're pretty sure it was some sort of shaft for one of the old mine workings. The whole mountain is riddled with them."

"Jesus," I said without thinking, "that could have been you."

"I know," Ricky responded. "I didn't realize how close a call it was until we were throwing those rocks down the hole."

"Do you think Rusty sensed the danger?" I said, my mystery book now totally forgotten in favor of what was obviously a better tale.

"I don't know," Ricky replied, "But I'm going to treat him a lot better from now on. There's no doubt that I was going to walk right across that snow patch. Rusty tangles with porcupines nearly every summer, so I don't think he's the smartest dog in the world, but he seemed to know there was some sort of danger there. I'm going to believe he was looking out for me."

"I know one thing," I said, picking my book

back up, "someone's looking out for you." But as I said this, I felt an unexpected, involuntary chill run through my entire body. It was August.

Not long after that, Ricky had the opportunity to square things up with Rusty. The Morrison family lived up the street from us and they owned a big, nasty brute of a dog that would rush, snarling viciously and throwing itself against their back gate, every time my brother walked by with Rusty, which was practically a daily occurrence. Both Ricky and Rusty just got used to it after a while and knowing my brother as I did I had little doubt that, on occasion he would make a point of goading the beast.

Then one day I was coming back from visiting with Marlene and found Ricky on the lawn in the back yard, swabbing our dog down with a wet cloth that he was soaking with water from the garden hose. I could see what looked like blood on the cloth, but didn't at first notice any on Rusty himself until I took a closer look. The blood was seeping from two deep looking gashes to the back of his neck, near where his collar was.

"What happened?" I said in panic as I knelt down beside the two of them. Rusty was panting and I could see slobber around his mouth and streaks of it across the bridge of his nose.

"That fucking dog of Morrison's just attacked him," my brother replied without taking his attention off his task. I could tell he'd been crying. "We were walking up the alley by their place and he ran and jumped on the back gate like he always does. Only this time someone must have been careless and left the gate unlatched. Next thing I knew that bastard was in the alley and had Rusty by the back of his neck and was shaking him like a rag. I didn't know what to do, so I kicked at him a few times, but he didn't seem to even notice I was there. He was insane. Then I spotted a banjo shovel leaning against the shed in the Morrison's yard. I ran over and grabbed it, ran back in the alley and hit the dog on the top of the head with it. I hit him so hard you could actually hear it make a bonging sound. He didn't let up on Rusty one little bit, so I hit him a second time and he still wouldn't let go. He was definitely there to kill. I took one last, big swing at him and brought it down on his head so hard I thought it would kill him. It should have, actually. Then he let Rusty go and turned on me. He was baring his teeth and it looked like he was going to come at me. I still had the shovel in my hands so I rammed the sharp blade right into his face. He let out a yelp and ran back into his yard. I latched the gate real quick, threw the shovel back in their yard and packed Rusty home."

I could see that my brother's hands were still shaking violently as he washed out our dog's wounds. "You could have been attacked yourself," I said weakly, knowing full well that standing by and watching as his dog was being killed by another would never have been an option for Ricky. I stroked Rusty's silky ears gently and put my arm around my brother's shoulder. "But you did the right thing."

"Good thing dad got that big thick studded collar for him last year," Ricky noted. "I think that may have been what saved his life."

"No," I replied. "I think you saved his life."

Our pooch recovered from the trauma in a few days. His wounds healed quickly, and my brother, in his wisdom, didn't walk up the alley with him anymore. About a year later the dog attacked and seriously bit the Town's meter reader. The Morrisons were firmly asked to have the dog put down and they complied.

Chapter 6

No One "Buys" A Dog

Dogs always played a part in our lives, and in the fabric of our neighborhood as well. Whether it was Perry Edwards' three-legged whatchamacallit to dear old Butch, fed and watered by the Baratoli family, who persisted in denying the dog was theirs almost until the day he died. Miraculously, Butch escaped capture by the local dogcatcher who made regular forays through our neighborhood searching out any dogs that were on the loose or without the requisite dog tag.

Butch could best be described as an outdoor dog. He just strayed into the neighborhood one day and stayed. To the consternation of the Baratoli family, their back yard was his favored hangout, but they got used to him after a while. No one came to claim him and little wonder. In spite of his gentle face, he wasn't much to look at. But then, nor were any of the other neighborhood dogs, truth be told. Even dear old Rusty whose appearance was deceptively close to that of a cocker spaniel was clearly not genetically uncontaminated.

They were all what we liked to call mongrel tough—proud metaphors for our neighborhood, I suppose. They had to be resilient because their life choices were severely limited. If they got sick or injured they could either get better on their own or die.

Don't get me wrong here. There probably wasn't a single boy in the neighborhood who was not completely attached to his trusty sidekick and, almost without exception, every boy had a dog.

The hard reality was that the nearest veterinarian was over thirty miles away in a neighboring town and most adults didn't feel the trip, nor its accompanying expense, was worth it. After all, nobody ever actually bought a dog in those days so replacing your lost pet was simply a matter of waiting to see what unfortunate neighbor ended up with an unwanted litter of puppies. This happened with regularity in the absence of spaying or neutering.

So when a boy would ask his parents for a dog,

he'd simply say, "Can we get a dog?" You would never hear him say something like, "Can we get a Golden Lab?" or, "Can we get a Dachshund?" That would have been just ridiculous. That would have cost money. Nobody bought a dog.

Somewhere along the way it fell upon our dad to be the unaccredited dog fixer-upper with the limited duties of extracting porcupine quills from the faces of Rusty, Butch and a number of other unfortunates. This happened with scrupulous regularity since the dogs in question were rugged but not blessed with stellar memories nor apparently, with any self-preservation instincts.

So with our mom's sewing scissors and a pair of needle-nose pliers it became a ritual every spring for the neighbors to bring over their pin-cushioned dogs and have our dad snip the tips off the quills and extract them with the pliers while the bereft owners held their squirming animals in place, simultaneously attempting to prevent a serious dog bite. Butch was, by far, the worst. He never seemed to develop the good sense to lay off those hated quilled adversaries. After a few years he simply took it upon himself to seek the medical attention he knew he'd get from our father. He'd just sit there and whine a bit while the rough surgery

was performed somehow knowing in his dog-brain
that it was for the best.

Chapter 7

No "Ticket to Ride"

Well, here we go. Ricky's in big trouble, yet again. He came home just before supper and looked an absolute fright. His face, his hair, his hands, everything was covered with coal dust. It hadn't been the first time, but this was somehow different, and with her laser instincts mom knew it, too. She questioned Ricky who, wise in the ways of his own self-preservation, admitted to the lesser misdeed of playing on the coal slack piles. After all, every kid in the Pass did that and could expect a mild scolding for it. Coal dirt was, after all, something we lived with every day. But mom knew it was something different this time just by the nature of the grime. Ricky hadn't quite worked his story out as well as he should have. She asked who he was with and it was at that point that he knew the lie had been foiled. He really did hate lying to mom, but the lie had already been concocted with his two co-horts so he had to stay with it or get them in trouble as well. So that's what he did. Telling on your friends was completely unconscionable. Your parents would probably forgive a lie, but your friends might never forgive a squealer.

"That's not the kind of dirty you get jumping off the coal slack piles," mom said in her most accusing tone. "I've seen you after you kids have done that. Remember? It's nothing like this. Look at your hair. Hair doesn't get like that from jumping off coal piles. You've even managed to get it in your eyes."

"I landed wrong and had to do a dive roll," Ricky countered. That didn't dissuade mom in her quest for the truth, but I could see already that my brother was simply going to dig his heels in and drive her to exasperation.

The whole thing went back and forth for at least another ten minutes and my brother's ploy won out, but not before our mother twisted the knife a little bit by laying on some well-measured guilt.

"I've never known you to lie to me like this before, Ricky. I'm ashamed of you."

I could tell that her words stabbed into him deeply, and I detected just the slightest bit of desire in him to come clean. But he didn't.

"Get out of those dirty clothes, go take a bath and get up to your bedroom," she finished, turning back to the stove to continue making supper.

If ever there was a Mexican standoff, this was it. Mom's only recourse was to wisely levy a punishment harsher than that warranted for the professed misdeed—the much-needed bath, no supper, banished to his room and grounded for the next weekend. It was just her way of letting Ricky know that he hadn't fooled her, while admitting to herself that she wasn't likely to get to the truth either. I could hardly wait until dishes were done to go upstairs and find out what really had happened and to sneak Ricky up a couple of sausages from the supper leftovers. I don't know why I was so kind to him. After all, and once again, I had been left alone to do all the dishes.

Using the sausages as my ploy to open the conversation I handed them to him, sat on the edge of the bed and led with, "So, cough it up. Mom's right. There's something else going on here."

He looked a little embarrassed and slightly reluctant to relate the events of the afternoon to me. "Don't you ever breathe a word of this to anyone," he warned after giving it some serious thought. "I only lied to mom to keep the other guys from getting into trouble. The problem around here is that all our moms know one another too well."

It was just like him to shift the burden of his actions onto someone or something else in order to salve his guilty conscience. The real culprits here, as it turns out, were actually mothers who talked to one another.

"Oh, here we go again," I said. "The ring of silence." But I didn't say more for fear he'd clam up with me as he had with mom.

"We were all just hanging around down at Crazy Joe's Pond when the coal train was going by," he said. "It was going really slow through town so we thought it would be a great idea to jump into one of the coal cars and take a ride to Bellevue. Then we could just hop off and walk or hitchhike back to town. All three of us managed to get into the same coal car. As soon as the train got out of Blairmore it really picked up speed. It was kind of fun at first, crouched down in the loaded coal car, but the coal dust began to blow around and all of us were getting really filthy. Then, when the train got to Bellevue, it didn't slow down at all like we expected it to and it was going way too fast to jump off. That's when we really started to get worried."

I think I said something like, "Ricky, you guys are imbeciles. I would have thought that after your history with trains you would have more sense than that."

"I just know that we weren't laughing anymore," he said. "As far as we knew, the next place the train might slow down or stop would be Lethbridge, then we'd be in real deep shit. We just had no choice but to stay hunched down in the coal car until it did. "We were getting dirtier and dirtier, but that was the least of our worries. For some unknown reason though, the train actually slowed down a bit at Burmis. We were surprised because there's really nothing at Burmis that it should have slowed down for, but we wasted no time climbing down to the bottom rung of the ladders and jumping off. Nick and Matt scraped themselves up pretty badly when they fell on the gravel, but at least we were off the train. "We walked up to the highway and tried to hitch a ride back. This guy actually stopped, but when we got to his car and he saw how dirty we all were he wouldn't give us a ride. We walked the five miles back to Bellevue and tried to clean ourselves up a bit in the gas station restroom there but it didn't help much. Then this guy with a half-ton came in to get gas and he gave us a ride back to Blairmore in the back of his truck."

Just two years earlier a young boy in Coleman barely survived when he tried to jump onto the side ladder of a train going through Bushtown. His feet had slipped off the ladder and he had both of his legs severed just below the knees when they swung under the train wheels as he fell. I closed my eyes and all I could picture was my brother, lying there on a hospital bed, two bandaged stumps where his legs should be.

This was the first time I actually gave Ricky a slap across the face. I was so angry it just happened before I knew it. He looked at me in total shock. Then my tears came and I hugged him through my blurred vision. He knew I loved him, the little bugger. And as much as I longed to tell mom the truth of the story, I again decided not to. My brother and I had this pact, y'know. More and more I began to feel that I was the one carrying the lion's share of

the load as he danced away, guiltless and unre-
morseful.

Chapter 8

The "Pane" Of It All

For whatever reason, geography played an important role in the fabric of youthful adventure—and misdeeds—in our hometown. I don't know if this was due to the great variety of terrain or the simple fact that said terrain provided a wealth of shelter from detection and a full range of escape routes. Where there's cover, there's trouble.

Dad had trimmed down a couple of the bigger poplar trees in our yard and the branches hadn't been hauled away yet. The previous summer our older brother, Walter, had shown Ricky the slingshot that he'd fashioned from the Y branch of a tree, rubber from a bicycle tube and the leather tongue from an old work boot.

Dad should have hauled those branches away sooner. It didn't take my brother long to find a branch with a crook in it just like Walter's. Getting the rubber and leather was no problem at all. Used bike tubes were hanging from nails in the shed and dad went through at least two pairs of work boots a year; the old ones often discarded under the cellar steps.

Three days later Ricky was testing his creation down in the creek bed near our place by firing stones against the creek's concrete retaining wall. One misdirected shot skimmed above the top of the wall, across the street, and right into the middle of a plate glass window in an old closed down neighborhood convenience store.

"I stood down there thinking nothing had happened," Ricky confessed to me. "It was just this little pop sound, but when I peeked up over the edge of the wall to take a look, I watched the whole window collapse into a million pieces. I ran like heck up the creek bed for about half a mile, then came out by the foot bridge and walked home like nothing happened."

In our quiet times together Ricky never really fibbed to me or made up stories that weren't true, and sure enough, when I walked by the store the next morning there were two fresh sheets of plywood over what used to be a window. As far as anyone was concerned, this mishap could just as easily have been attributed to a vehicle going by and spitting a rock from its tire. One thing was certain, though. Keeping my mouth shut was becoming a habit. I actually thought about asking my brother not to confide in me anymore, but I just couldn't imagine living with the boredom that would have visited upon me.

Chapter 9

200 Pounds of Rolling Mayhem

The window incident paled in comparison to the tire one, however. My friend, Anna, and I were at the swings in the park at the old Shale Pit on a Saturday afternoon just doing what girlfriends do, swinging side by side and chatting about whatever came to mind. Now this is where geography, once again, plays an important role as I noted earlier.

The shale pit was a now-abandoned excavation into the side of a hill at the southeast edge of town. The shale had been used in the early days for the town's roads and pathways. Above and further to the south of the pit was the town dump. Built into the pit was a small park that included a ball diamond complete with wood and chicken wire backstop. Behind the backstop was a street, then a row of older homes.

"What the heck's going on up there?" Anna

said as she gazed up at the rim of the pit. I didn't have time to answer. Even though we were well away from its path both of us looked on in horror as this huge tractor tire careened down the steep face of the shale pit, bounced wildly across the ball diamond outfield, smashed into the backstop splintering the wood like kindling and kept right on going. Barely losing any of its momentum, the tire shot across the road and, like a guided missile, it smashed squarely into the front door of the house directly across the street knocking the door clean off its hinges.

We sat there on the swings looking in astonishment over our shoulders at the now door-less house. No one came out. We quickly reached the optimistic conclusion that no one was home. It never dawned on us for a second that someone in the house might have been mortally injured. "Let's get out of here now before we get blamed for this," Anna said. I took a quick glance back up at the rim of the pit. The three culprits had disappeared. A terrible thought crossed my mind, but I immediately dismissed it.

"Yes," I agreed, "let's go." Innocent or guilty, it was always a good idea to get as far away as possible from things like this. Maybe there really was some logic in my brother's thinking after all. How little did I know.

So that was that. A funny story to tell all the other girls in school on Monday. Kids had been rolling small tires down the back of the shale pit and into the ball diamond backstop for as long as I could remember. With the town dump being so close there was always a ready supply of discarded tires to choose from and generally the backstop did its job, though a little the worse for wear.

"You won't believe what happened today," Ricky said. We were walking back together from Catonio's neighborhood store where mom had sent us to get a few grocery items for supper.

Without a second thought, I said, "Oh brother, don't tell me it was you. Was it you guys that rolled that huge tire down the shale pit this afternoon?"

By the tone of my voice Ricky panicked, thinking the news might have gone all over town and already made it back to his own sister. The fear was visible in his eyes because he knew, as did all the neighborhood kids, that if something really serious had happened, like someone been badly injured or even killed, he and his buddies would be first in line to be questioned by the police. The cops might be around anyway. The house was without a door and by anybody's rule book, that was vandalism.

"Who told you?"

"No one," I replied. "Anna and I were at the swings when that tire came down. Then we took off before we got blamed for anything."

Fear still showing clearly on him Ricky owned up to the deed and, once again, swore me to silence.

"When we saw the tire go through the door we ran like crazy," he said. "We found that huge tractor tire and thought it would be neat to see how it went down the hill. We really thought the backstop would stop it, but it didn't even slow the tire down. We thought it was funny until it took the door off. Then we panicked."

"So you rocket scientists thought a bigger tire might somehow roll down the hill differently than a small one?" I commented sardonically, not truly expecting any sort of intelligent response. The only other question I could muster to this confession was, "And who's we?"

"It was Nick, Matt and me," he confided. I just rolled my eyes. I knew it. Why did I even ask?

There were well over a dozen of the little trou-
blemakers in our neighborhood who could have
done this and the police would have no problem at
all putting together a list of likely suspects. With
absolute certainty any combination of this group
was somehow involved but getting that combination right was the real difficult task. It seemed to
me, though, that Ricky was always the common
element, but he seemed to always slip under the ra-
dar.

"It is not the strongest of the species that survive, nor the most intelligent, but the one most re-
sponsive to change." Charles Darwin said that. At
home we were taught the theory of evolution in
much the same manner as our Catholic friends
learned about Adam and Eve. The truth of Darwin's statement became clear to me when I realized
how effortlessly my brother moved within his environment and how he actually seemed to fashion
that environment around him to suit his needs.
That's why he was seldom caught up in anything.
He was neither a creature of habit nor one to con-
form to set routine. It definitely kept him out of
trouble. A few of the neighborhood kids had done
stints in reform school for a variety of juvenile offences, but that wasn't ever to be my brother's

fate.

So we never really knew why, but in spite of his very real fears, nothing ever came of the tire incident. Though this was markedly different due to the size of the tire and the damage it had done, rolling tires down a steep hill could hardly have been that high on the list of things the police wanted to investigate. There had been damage, that was for sure, but no one had been injured or killed.

Chapter 10

So Where Did He Get To Now?

Not everything that happened to Ricky was within his control or his fault. The First Annual Blairmore Winter Carnival in the town's new arena is one incident that is a case in point.

The carnival was a really big deal, marking the opening of Blairmore's brand new ice arena. A number of the organizers thought it a great idea to have teams of local youth do an on-ice equivalent of the Calgary Stampede Chuck Wagon Races. The chuck wagons were specially rigged up toboggans, each pulled by a team of six kids on skates, two outriders behind with ropes to keep the toboggans from swinging out of control on the corners, and, of course, a driver. They did a pretty good job because short of no wheels the toboggans really looked like chuck wagons, complete with canopies made from donated white bed sheets.

The objective, like the real chuck wagon races, was to finish the figure eight course first in a field of six teams. Naturally, Ricky found himself on one of the teams, and because he was the smallest and lightest, he was given the somewhat honorary role of driver.

At the whistle all six teams took off, and the mayhem began. Teams got tangled up. Kids were falling everywhere and you couldn't tell one group from another at about the halfway mark. Then incredibly, Ricky's team emerged from the mess ahead of the rest of them. Just before they rounded the last corner of the figure eight both of his outriders collided with each other, fell on the ice and let go of their ropes.

On the corner the toboggan with Ricky on the reins careened wildly out of control and slammed sideways into the boards. The collision could be heard throughout the packed arena. Undaunted, the team continued on and dashed over the finish line with the toboggan laying on its side and Ricky still hanging on to it for dear life. They'd won.

The ribbon and trophy presentation followed, but missing from the winning team line-up was my brother. No one could find him. He'd simply disappeared. Mom and dad went home after the race, but I stayed behind with a few of my girlfriends to take in the rest of the festivities.

When I finally got home Ricky was up in his bedroom laying on his bed and looking seriously green around the gills. Mom had put a puke bucket beside his bed with the requisite two or three inches of water in the bottom. I didn't linger too long looking at its contents. "What happened to you this afternoon?" I asked. "You guys won the race and you missed out on getting your ribbon and your picture taken for the newspaper."

"Mom didn't tell you?" he responded weakly.

"Tell me what?" I asked.

"Well, I guess I might as well then," he moaned. "I think I ate a bad hotdog or something this afternoon, and I was feeling really sick when I got on the toboggan. But I couldn't let the rest of the team down. I was OK until we went into that last corner and the toboggan slammed into the boards. It hit so hard that I, uh, well," he paused, "well, I shit my pants. And it wasn't just a little, either. It's a good thing mom made me wear those thermal long johns or you would have been able to follow me all the way home. As soon as we got over the finish line I got out of the toboggan and I had

81

to get out of there. I ran straight home and had to stop two or three times to puke. "Don't you tell anyone, or I'll kill you. Mom and dad came home a bit later and mom took care of the mess, and believe me, it was a mess."

Ricky looked miserable lying there on his bed still obviously sicker than a dog. And, as much as I tried not to, I laughed uncontrollably for the next half an hour. And for the next few days, whenever I pictured him going over the finish line with the toboggan tipped on its side and my brother with his pants full, I just broke out laughing all over again. There were several times after that when Ricky provided me with ample reason not to, but I kept his embarrassing secret. I can't speak for our mom and dad, but I think they did, too.

It was four or five years later before my brother even attempted to eat another hotdog, and after gagging on the first bite it was added to his rather short list of foods he refused to eat right next to canned peas, salted codfish and tapioca pudding.

Chapter 11

A Winter Wonderland

I always hated winters. Probably because I wasn't much into sports—particularly winter sports—and didn't embrace the cold season like my brother and all of his buddies did. Mom got me into figure skating for a few years, but I hated it. She thought I looked cute with my little skirted costume at the annual figure skating carnival, but she soon realized that I didn't share her enthusiasm and let me drop out.

I wasn't that good at it anyway. I began skating with some normal skates that had regular blades just like the boys' skates. But when I got into figure skating my parents had to invest in a pair of real figure skates; the ones with the serrated picks on the front and similar in no way to the ones that I'd learned to skate on. I appreciated that my new skates didn't have that ugly white, childish furry stuff around the tops, but that was short-lived.

The first time on the ice with my new blades the picks dug in and I fell flat on my face. Having skated for a full year with regular blades I was definitely having difficulty adapting to my new ones, which required a completely different technique. I continued to do face plants and actually hurt myself a few times when I fell hard on the ice.

Dad saw that I was having real difficulty and felt really sorry for me, so instead of allowing me more time to adapt he had his own solution. He always had his own solutions to things, bless his heart. The next morning, he took my skates to work with him and ground the bottom pick off each skate with his bench grinder.

I have to admit that the alteration worked well in that I stopped tripping. The problem was, figure skates were built like that for a reason, and that bottom pick was not just arbitrarily put there to make little girls trip and fall. My figure skating coach could never understand why I simply could not master some of the most basic skating maneuvers. I just shrugged, but never did let her know about the alterations my father had made. Truthfully, I didn't realize until later that this had been the chief reason for all my difficulties.

Two years later dad took the skates to the arena and gave them to the figure skating instructor to donate to one of the younger girls coming up. The instructor took one look at the blades and asked dad, "What happened here? The bottom pick is completely missing on both skates." Dad admitted to what he'd done and, thanking him for his generosity, she handed them back to him. "Maybe you should buy a new pair for Kathryn and get her back into figure skating," she suggested. I never did go back.

My winters were limited to the occasional day of tobogganing; those days being when temperatures rose to just under the freezing mark. I couldn't tolerate the cold and the snow. In spite of my parents' promptings, I was happiest curled up on my bed with a good book on those cold winter days.

Ricky and his buddies loved it all. The temperature would have to drop to nearly 30 below before any of them would even consider the logical option of staying indoors.

Winters were just one continuous round of league hockey, road hockey, tobogganing, skiing, snow fort building and virtually anything else that could be done in the snow or on ice.

What I'm about to tell you next may leave you thinking that parents/adults back then were totally irresponsible when it came to child rearing, and for certain there were tragedies for which one could make a strong case for a lack of parental oversight. Truth is, you can't watch over your children all the time, and bad things are always going to happen. Close calls were generally the order of the day though, rather than outright catastrophes.

Chapter 12

What Goes Up, Must Come Down...
Right?

Blairmore always had a ski hill, at least as far back as I can remember. Its history went way back to the 1930s when a group of local volunteers slashed out a wide swath to the top of the tall bluff on the south side of town and eventually equipped it with a rope tow. It wasn't much, but in the 1950s and 60s it was enough of a hill to draw the occasional weekend bus tour from the metropolis of Lethbridge, 80 miles to the east of the Pass.

The homemade rope tow was powered by a motor and transmission from an old truck. The hill was always operated by local volunteers who early, early on had seen fit to build a small, one-room log lodge at the bottom of the hill heated by a huge potbelly stove. In its heyday the lodge even had a concession counter that ran on a less than regular basis, so it was important that you brought your own sandwiches to the hill if you expected to eat.

I never skied myself, but I did go over to the hill a few times at my brother's urging to watch their daredevil ski antics, which invariably were less spectacular from a spectator's point of view than the performer's. However, I must admit that the lodge was pretty comfy. The big potbelly stove cast warmth to every corner and there was the ever-present, but not unpleasant, smell of melting ski wax mixed with the distinct odor of wool mittens drying on the stovetop. The entire side of the lodge that faced the ski hill was fitted with small-paned glass windows affording a view of the skiers from its cabin-like cozy comfort. And on a good day, you might even be able to buy a hot chocolate at the volunteer-run concession.

During the Christmas school break a small circle of neighborhood boys, which naturally included my brother as well as his friend, Bruce Fairweather, were allowed to use the ski hill during the weekdays without adult supervision. This was due, in no small measure, to the fact that Bruce's dad, one of the town's two lawyers, was president of the ski hill volunteer committee and thought of his boy as being exceptionally responsible. The real bonus, though, was that Bruce's dad also gave him the key to the tow shack along with the ignition key to the rope tow motor.

Mr. Fairweather had the foresight to extract a promise from Bruce that the boys would hike up and check out the rope tow's safety gate at the top of the hill before using it. The safety gate was little more than an extension cord that ran across the path of the rope at the top of the hill, placed between where the skiers dismounted at the top and the lift's big four-foot diameter bull wheel. It worked on the simple principle that if a skier failed to dismount and went across the extension cord it simply pulled the plug out and shut off the tow motor before the skier got anywhere near the dangerous bull wheel. Simple, but effective... usually.

But boys are inherently lazy and anything that postpones or delays their playtime must be dealt with expeditiously. Though Bruce had been told to check the safety gate, there certainly had to be an easier and quicker way of doing it. It had snowed almost fourteen inches the night before, so all eight of the boys gathered there that morning were anxious to get to the top of the hill and start skiing in all of that fresh powder.

This was going to be a perfect day for schussing, which for those not familiar with downhill skiing is the practice of going straight down the hill, no turning and no stopping. That much fresh snow would ensure that they could schuss from top to bottom without the worry of reaching speeds that most assuredly would result in bodily harm.

Needless to say, they were all far less anxious to go slogging to the top of the hill in that same deep snow to check out something that was probably working okay anyway. The problem: these were exactly the conditions that required such caution.

It didn't take long to come up with Plan B. Bruce would run the tow real slow and a few of the guys would jump on and ride rather than hike to the top of the hill and check the gate out. Ricky volunteered to lead the way, with two others right behind to help pull the rope out of several low spots on the tow path where it would invariably have been buried under the fresh layer of new snow.

As the rope slowly pulled them up the hill Ricky crouched and used the crook of his leg to help lift the buried sections of the rope out of the heavy snow. The jute rope twisted and twanged under the tension as it was pulled from the snow.

When Ricky got to the dismount spot at the top he was horrified to find that the rope had twisted enough to wrap a grip on his loose-fitting coat and one of his woolen mitts. Added to that was the fact that the rope itself had sprung out of the deep snow at the top, but the safety gate remained buried beneath. Ricky's skis ran right over the top of the buried extension cord and the tow just kept right on running. He fell down in a futile effort to free himself. The tow dragged him another twenty feet, and as it rose to meet the elevated bull wheel, it finally let the coat and Ricky loose. Not his mitt, though. It came off Ricky's hand and stayed stuck to the rope as it went around the wheel, got seriously mangled up and began its return trip to the bottom of the hill.

Ricky lay in the snow for a long while, the pocket of his new ski coat chewed and ripped and missing one much-needed mitt. It was a long, cold, miserable trip back to the bottom of the hill but a lesson burned by terror into his brain. He had seen what the bull wheel had done to his mitt, and imagined what it would have done to him had he not gotten himself free.

Explaining the torn coat, Ricky told mom that he had accidentally caught it on a tree branch, but once again, something told me there was a bit more to the story, and Ricky gave it up to me later once more accompanied by my sworn oath of silence. Typically, he had forgotten how close he'd come to death or injury and was more concerned that the story would get out and he and his pals would lose their ski hill privileges which no doubt would have been the case.

* * *

Ricky's other, less fantastical ski hill stories often had me laughing to tears. He and his occasional ski pal, Ronny Hallak, were joking about the Sunday morning a busload of skiers from Lethbridge arrived at the hill. Once geared up everyone queued up to take the tow up the hill. According to Ronny one of the Lethbridge ladies got to the front of the lift line, carefully edged her way up to the rope, then grabbed on in a death grip, rather than easing on gently.

"That must have been her first time," Ronny laughed. "The rope yanked her clean out of her ski boots. She wouldn't let go, and the rope dragged her fifty yards up the hill in her sock feet before the operator could stop it. She wasn't really hurt, and everyone in the line had a good laugh looking at her two skis sitting there perfectly together with the ski boots still attached to them and her walking back down in her sock feet." Safety bindings had actually been invented by then but were not in wide usage, so those lace-up leather boots were staying with their skis, held fast by the cable harnesses.

* * *

The rope tow transmission had three gears just like the truck it came from, and Ricky and Ronny used to joke that on the days when they could use the hill unsupervised Bruce Fairweather would often get the tow into third gear. The challenge for the guys was to get down the hill as fast as they could get up. "When you could finally get a full grip on the rope, which took some serious effort, it felt like you were doing about twenty-five miles an hour," Ricky told me.

I found out as the years went by, that my brother often chose to downplay things when relating them to me. I think he was trying to avoid another slap across the side of his head or an outburst of tears, all of which depended upon the severity of his misdeed.

He delighted from time to time in relating, with that big stupid grin on his face, the misadventures of his pals. I think he felt that if I knew that he wasn't the only one getting into hot water, I would be more accepting of the fact that he garnered significantly more than his share.

Chapter 13

Shake It Down

Ricky and I were walking to school together one morning, which seldom happens since he's usually with two or three of the gang. Tromping through the new snow, that all-to-familiar grin told me to brace myself for his post-mortem of the weekend.

During the winter months he and five or six of his friends, including Chris Santoro, had the enviable and much sought-after job of being rink rats at the arena. That meant cleaning and flooding the skating ice and any other sundry duties that were required to keep the rink in shape. No money was involved. In return for their efforts the boys got to use the rink nearly every unscheduled Saturday afternoon to play hockey and they were occasionally treated to a pop or chocolate bar from the arena concession. They got the job less for their stellar work ethic than for the fact that the arena's manager was Amelio Santoro, Chris's dad.

I should note here that Amelio was almost as famous for his hot temper as our own father was. That was not helped by the fact that he regularly had to take charge of a crew of pre-pubescent boys who possessed the collective good judgment of a fence post.

"So, last Saturday morning," Ricky related to me, with that almost ever-present smirk of his, "our jobs for the morning were to flood the skating rink and replace a few of the burned out light bulbs over the ice. "After the ice was flooded, Chris, me, and a few of the other guys slid the big fourteen-foot wooden stepladder across it to the nearest light that needed a new bulb. Chris went up the ladder with the bulb, unscrewed the old one and reached up to put the new one in its place. It slipped from his hand, fell to the ice and shattered into a thousand shards of glass. "Amelio, over at the edge of the rink, saw the whole thing go down, and completely lost his mind. We're all pretty used to his regular outbursts, but this was something special. "As he came across the ice to the ladder and saw all the broken glass it got even worse and we all headed for safety and out of the danger zone.

Except for poor Chris; he was still up at the top of that ladder with his dad below screaming at him like a madman, and as far as Chris was concerned, he was going to stay up there until his dad's temper cooled down. That made Amelio even madder, and he began to violently shake the ladder.

"We all stood away, completely terrified," said Ricky. "Chris was up at the very top clinging on for his life. If he fell from there he probably would have really hurt himself. Fortunately for him, his dad's temper cooled down almost as quickly as it had flared up. He hadn't mellowed out, or anything like that; it's just that he had passed through the homicidal stage. A good thing, too," Ricky added, "because Chris couldn't have held on up there very much longer.

"We were all pretty quiet after that. Amelio was still just barely controlling himself. He barked at us to clean up the broken glass, replace the bulb and re-flood that area of the ice; then he just stomped off to the compressor room."

"You mean the decompressor room," I interrupted in a sorry attempt at humor. Ricky looked at me oddly and didn't seem to get it. He went on with his story.

"We all stood there under the ladder, then Chris realized that the replacement light bulbs were kept in that compressor room. We bushed to see which one of us would have to go in there and fetch the new bulb. Matt lost, so we all jokingly shook hands with him, bid him farewell, and told him it was nice knowing him, as though we'd never see him again. Matt came back about ten minutes later with the new bulb in one hand and three hockey pucks in the other."

"'Where'd you get those from?' we all asked almost in unison.

"'Your dad gave them to me,' Matt replied directing his comment to Chris. 'He found them under the bleachers after that big game last night.'

"Amelio had obviously cooled off... a lot. Either that or he was sending a message to Chris that, son or not, he was not on the top of his list of favorite rink rats."

As could be expected from this bunch, the terror brought on by the moment didn't last too long. On their way home the boys couldn't resist teasing Chris about his predicament up on the ladder and the fact that his own dad was the perpetrator.

"Nick commented to Chris that he looked

pretty 'shook up' when he was clinging to the top of the ladder, to which he replied that it was a hell of a lot better than being shook down," Ricky quipped.

I thought, "You find that funny and you completely missed my decompressor room joke."

One of the big problems with that whole crew was that they never took anything seriously for very long. They always seemed to find the seed of humor in everything they did regardless of how grave the circumstance. It would take something incredibly devastating to change that. Unfortunately, that was not far off.

Chapter 14

Life Among The "Tree People"

It seemed like a lot of things in Ricky's life involved heights. Maybe it was because we lived in the mountains. I never had a thing for high places, but most of the boys did with the rare exception of a very few who had an inherent fear of them. Ricky was not one of those. Nor, in fact, were many of those he hung with.

The boys all spent countless hours in the summer and every weekend in the bush. They fished, they swam, they hiked and they built countless cabins which amounted to little more than lean-tos and other tent-like affairs. Most were built with chopped down jack pines covered with pine boughs. They were pretty rough at best, but the quality of these poor structures was due to the lack of any really good building materials laying around for ready use.

One summer they all decided that it might be a good idea to build a tree house or two right in town. Why not? The town was in a construction boom and all sorts of old lumber and discarded building materials were laying around just for the taking. Surely none of the contractors would miss a 2 by 8 or two or a few scraps of plywood. And, what self-respecting father back then didn't have a hoard of nails ranging from one inch finishing to eight-inch spikes?

So the projects began. The first task was to choose some suitable trees on unused land which was no big deal since the town was full of old-growth cottonwoods and tons of open spaces. Ricky and his crew chose a spot by Lyons Creek near the old library and next to Spring Pond.

"Why are you guys building it up in the trees?" I questioned. "Wouldn't it be simpler to just build it down on the ground?"

Ricky gave me a pained look, as though that was about the dumbest question he'd ever heard. He couldn't even dignify it with a response and walked away shaking his head.

Spring Pond was somewhat of a mini-version of Crazy Joe's Pond, which lay about half a mile east of it. Both were little more than spring runoff catch basins which filled with water in the spring and were almost totally dried up by late summer. Crazy Joe's was large enough to raft on in the spring and early summer and it was the bane of existence for the CPR whose rail line ran right past it. Most of the rafts that were built by the local kids were constructed of a few boards or plywood nailed across three or four wooden CPR replacement rail ties. It eventually became apparent to the CPR that dropping off the ties by the railway in advance of future replacement was not a good idea. Few of them made it to their intended purpose as noted by the sheer number of ties that had, over time, become waterlogged and were lying at the bottom of the pond.

But we're getting a bit off topic here.

Anyway, it took a few days of stealth and minor larceny, but Ricky and crew scavenged enough lumber to at least get a start on their tree house. The best tree prospect had been three cottonwoods growing fairly close together, so the structure was to be three rather than four-sided and positioned at a height somewhere between fifteen and twenty feet.

"How's the tree fort coming along?" I asked

him after they'd been at it a few days.

"Don't call it a fort," he shot back at me. "That makes it sound like some little kid thing. It's just about done, actually. All we have to do now is put the roof on."

"So, until that's done it's a fort," I joked, unable to resist getting a little dig in. His dismissal of my wit was disappointing leaving me to assume that it had somehow, once again, gone over his head.

To them it was a labor of love and probably the first time any of them had built anything of any significance. They'd all worked every day on it, almost non-stop, and from three blocks away you could see this rather unsightly monstrosity taking shape. Some townspeople even came around to see what the heck it was.

"The hardest part was getting the platform built," my brother explained. "Once we had that up the rest was easy. We had all three walls nailed up in one day. The roof should be on this week. Then we'll be ready to move in."

"It looked pretty dangerous, you guys working way up there in the trees," I commented honestly. "Especially before you got the floor built. You guys looked like a bunch of monkeys."

"We had a few close calls," Ricky replied. "But, Benny Di Cenzo was the only guy who got hurt."

More than anything else he had said, Ricky's last sentence struck me.

"Benny got hurt?" I said. "Badly?"

"Naw, not really. He was just being an idiot, but it could have been worse, I guess," my brother replied in a tone that let me know he wasn't about to volunteer much more information.

I was left with no alternative but to ply him for the rest of the story, and it unfolded, ever so slowly, as was my brother's fashion when he sensed any sort of heightened curiosity on my part.

"A few of the cottonwood branches had to be cut to make way for the walls, and removing them was left to Benny," Ricky said. "He was the junior guy on the team, so we gave him some of the crappier jobs to do. Plus, he brought his dad's heavy-duty crosscut saw to the project. What Benny did can only be compared to something you might see in a Wiley Coyote/Roadrunner Cartoon. He sat on the branch he was cutting. Holding onto a smaller branch above him with his free hand he began sawing the branch he was sitting on, cutting between himself and the trunk of the tree. About halfway through the branch broke under his weight, and he couldn't keep his grip on the branch above. Down went Benny, landing ass first on the pile of remaining assorted lumber we had gathered."

"Aww, come on," I said, slapping my brother playfully on the shoulder. "No one's that stupid."

"Benny is. He's lucky we're lazy," Ricky went on, pausing now for effect.

"Okay, okay, why is he lucky that you guys are lazy?" I always hated when he baited me like this, and I knew he loved every minute of it, the little shit.

"Well, the fact that the lumber had been strewn, helter-skelter like a beaver dam probably saved him from serious injury, acting a bit like a springboard rather than a solid landing," Ricky explained. "When he landed on the pile he bounced off like it was a trampoline. What was more miraculous was the fact that many of those salvaged boards were full of rusty bent nails, and Benny missed every one of them."

After Ricky had told me the story, I thought he might have been making it up. No one could have been dumb enough to do what Benny had done, could they? But, truth is often stranger than fiction, so they say. Not wanting to challenge my brother's account of the incident, I quietly made a point of checking it out with Matt and Nick. I even brought it up with Benny himself thinking it would be nice to offer him the opportunity to rebut such a ridiculous tale.

The boys weren't making up a story. Benny's blush confirmed it.

The tree house summer was not to have a happy ending. Another group of Ricky's buddies had built a second one, five or six blocks away at the gravel storage yard used by the Town crew. The almost overnight presence of the two rather bizarre tree structures could not miss the watchful eyes of the town fathers who, while expressing respect for the engineering acumen of the builders, nonetheless ordered that they be removed. The structures were deemed unsightly, and in what was to turn out be a sadly ironic twist—unsafe.

My brother and his crew were on the demolition almost immediately due largely to the fact that our dad just happened to be one of those town fathers at the time and delivered the council's directive directly—if you get my drift.

"If dad wasn't on town council we would have just ignored them and made the town crew rip it down themselves," Ricky protested to me in a display of youthful defiance.

The tree house was gone within a day, but in one last act of disobedience, the boys left one of the 2 by 8 floor support boards nailed to the tree, a wistful reminder, I suppose, of their fleeting achievement. They had used their tree house for only three or four days. The board remained there for years.

The friends who had built the second tree house didn't get on their tear down for another week, and it was to have a terribly tragic end. When they had built their tree house they had put their trap door in the roof. Additionally, and since the gravel pile was right there, they decided it was a good idea to build a 2 by 4 wood retaining lip on the roof and fill it with gravel to weatherproof the structure; something they all agreed was a great idea. My brother and his crew, in fact, had expressed a little jealousy that their friend, Stevie Baldwin, and his team had had the gravel readily available to them.

Using it would turn out to be a decision with fatal consequences.

When the boys finally got on their demolition, their first task was to knock out all four walls, leaving the deck and roof intact. With nearly half a ton of gravel on it the support beams alone could not hold the extreme weight of the roof and it dropped like a guillotine. Stevie was the lucky one. He was standing directly under the open trap door and didn't move an inch as the entire roof collapsed around him. He came through untouched. Craig Andersen, one of the other friends, wasn't that lucky. Sensing that the roof was coming down, he tried to jump to the ground from the deck. The roof caught him in flight and he was left gruesomely and fatally hanging there, his head caught between the deck and the collapsed roof.

In the milieu of youthful exuberance and irresponsibility are the accompanying elements of tragedy and sadness. I had not known Craig as well as I did some of Ricky's closer friends, but the tragedy brought down on me a more profound, persistent anxiety than one might imagine. I could neither understand nor explain it, and worse, I could not escape it.

Something deeper, something more visceral, was triggered in me by his death, and it felt as unsettling as a cold wind on a warm summer day.

While my brother and the others mourned their loss, and then rather quickly assumed their normal lives again, I remained in this despondent state for several more weeks.

Chapter 15

I'm Hit, I'm Hit

Why can I laugh when I'm sad? I may never know, but I sometimes feel that Ricky can connect with my gloom and do and say all the right things to bring me around—temporarily, at least. By now he knew, or at least should have, that I longed for his tales, like he himself might enjoy reading The Adventures of Huckleberry Finn or Tom Sawyer. The only difference was, of course, that my brother's weren't fiction.

Tonight he was gleefully relating a brand new tale of the guys out target practicing with their .22s at the upper shale pit, which was accessed by an abandoned and mostly overgrown old road just south of town. The pit itself had not been used in decades. Because it was little more than an exca-vation into a steep hillside it was a favorite spot for target practicing as it provided a ready-made backstop. If you didn't know it was there you would likely never find it, but every boy who grew up in that corner of town knew how to get there. The guys had gathered up a batch of old tin cans and a few bottles from the town dump to use as targets and had packed them up there in an old burlap potato sack.

All of the guys except for Ricky owned .22 rifles. Dad, who as I noted earlier hadn't let any of his kids have a gun, had relaxed his rule enough to allow Ricky a CO_2 pellet rifle. Up at the shale pit the boys had set up the cans and bottles on the steep shale slope and set themselves up on the other ridge of the pit to shoot at them. After about twenty minutes of shooting it was time to reset the cans. All of the bottles by then had been broken.

It was Stevie's turn to set up the targets. Begrudgingly down he went then up the other side to set them up. That day Stevie was wearing his sheepskin vest. It was seriously thick with the skin outside and a heavy sheep's fleece lining the inside. He was a big boy and from the back, in his sheepskin vest, he looked like a bear.

"I don't really know whose brain wave it was," said Ricky, "but we decided to pull a fast one on Stevie. We all decided it would be a great idea if I shot him in the back with a pellet which certainly wouldn't penetrate the sheepskin. Nick would fire a shot in the air with his .22, which was noisier, right at the very same time."

And so, according to plan, that's exactly what they did without even the benefit of second thought. After all, why spoil such a fantastic prank by considering its possible negative consequences?

"When Stevie felt the sting of the pellet in his back and heard the .22 go off at the same time he fell back, yelling, 'I'm hit, I'm hit'. Then he rolled down fifteen or twenty feet to the bottom of the shale pit," Ricky said between chuckles. "We were all laughing like crazy and it took Stevie a fair bit of time to figure out what had really happened and that he was okay even after he saw us all laughing at him. He quickly took his vest off to check for a bullet hole in the back. He was thoroughly pissed off with all of us and we were almost back home before he began seeing any of the humor in it at all."

I slapped Ricky full force on his chest with both my hands setting him back a foot or more.

"Stevie? Of all the guys to do it to you idiots picked Stevie?" I yelped. "You all know he's got that heart condition. You might have given him a heart attack. Did you even think of that? Did it ever dawn on you that had Stevie had a heart attack, you—not your buddies, but you—would be held responsible since you fired the shot that hit him?"

"We really didn't think about that," Ricky admitted. "It's just that he was wearing that sheepskin, so we knew the pellet wouldn't really hurt him."

"Oh, of course. What was I thinking?" I responded in frustration.

I just threw up my hands in resignation and went back to my room to read. It gave me pause to reflect on things, most specifically those things that make boys tick; the things that make them different from girls. It wasn't so much that they conjured up such an evil little practical joke on the spur of the moment. No, that wasn't it at all. Girls have been known to do that, too. What struck me was the fact that Stevie's first reaction on realizing he was the brunt of the joke was one of embarrassment. Once he recovered from his embarrassment-induced anger he could smile and conjoin with the others in equal enjoyment of the prank. I just couldn't imagine myself, or any of my girlfriends, for that matter, being quite so magnanimous.

Chapter 16

The Voice of an Angel

By my words one might be left with the impression that my brother was little more than a walking bundle of melodrama. He was that, of course, but he was so much more. In as much as it irritated me, particularly on our frequent family car rides, he was always singing. He had a wonderful and powerful little boy singing voice.

His vocal talents were recognized early by Mr. Leighton, our elementary school's elderly white haired music teacher, who gave my brother extra attention each spring in preparation for the town's annual Lions Club Music Festival. My brother and a few of the other boys who were competing went over to Mr. Leighton's apartment above Kubik's Department Store after supper a few times prior to the festival for some extra practice.

Returning after one such visit Ricky said to me, "Mr. Leighton has a huge grand piano in that tiny, little apartment of his. He doesn't have a sofa or anything else in his living room; just that huge piano. There's hardly room to walk around it. I don't understand it. He doesn't even own a car and from the looks of his apartment he doesn't have much else, either."

"Mr. Leighton lives for his music," I said. "He's been teaching at the school forever and maybe, just maybe, he doesn't need much else. His piano and his music are what make him happy. Plus, he loves his students. What makes you think he needs anything more?"

"Oh, nothing really. It's just that everyone else I know has stuff. He doesn't."

My brother's concern for his music teacher's financial wellbeing may have arisen from his growing affection for him. He had a strange way of expressing himself in that regard, never actually coming right out and saying exactly how he felt. I knew, though. Ricky always showed respect to those adults he was particularly fond of. It had always been Mr. Leighton and never Old Man Leighton.

Ricky won first place honors in his age category

every year that he competed in vocals, always scoring in the high 80's. In what was to be his final year of competition he shared a gigantic trophy with an adult singer from a neighboring town for first place overall in male vocals. More importantly, he got the honor of singing in the festival's grand concert held the last evening of the week-long event. Mr. Leighton was accompanying him on the piano; a somewhat smaller one than that in his own apartment.

"When I went up on stage to sing I was shaking like a leaf," Ricky admitted to me. "The hall was full of people, not like during the competitions. I didn't realize how big the crowd was until I got on stage. Mr. Leighton was already sitting at his piano waiting for me and signaled for me to come over to him.

"When I got there he said to me, 'Are you nervous?'

"I just nodded my head stiffly and I said to him, 'Yeah, there's a lot of people out there. Are you nervous?'

"He gave me his big, warm smile and nodded back. His hands were on his lap and when I looked down at them I could see they were shaking just like mine were. He wasn't kidding me. 'You're the first student I've ever had that's made the grand concert,' he whispered to me.

"I looked at him in disbelief, but I realized it was true from the pride reflecting in his eyes. I knew then that we were sharing much more than just the stage. Glancing out at the audience, he said, 'We can keep 'em waiting a bit while we both settle down. Are your mom and dad here tonight?'

"I nodded again, and he said, 'Good. You'll need their help to take that big trophy home with you tonight. You ready? Let's do this thing.'

"I walked back the center of the stage, completely calm and at ease now. He looked over his shoulder at me from the piano, I gave him the little nod that I was ready and we did it. When it was over he stood up and began clapping. So did the audience. He walked over to me, put his hand on my shoulder and we took our bows together."

"Oh Ricky, how can you be such a moron one moment and something completely different the next?" I said, stifling back my own tears.

That was to be the last year my brother sang in the festival. The following year in the early stages of puberty his voice began to crack and change —

baritone one moment, falsetto the next and everything in between — sometimes all in one verse of a song. It was something that all kids go through at that stage of their lives, but it had a greater effect on my brother than most. Sadly, he never returned to competitive singing once his voice finally settled down, though the music festival went on for years after.

Mr. Leighton retired two years later and passed away from cancer not long after. Ricky and I went to his funeral. The church was filled to capacity. I looked over at my brother sitting next to me in the pew, and for the very first time ever I saw tears of real emotion. I leaned over to him and remembering back to our three-year-old conversation said, "Well, will you look at this. And you thought Mr. Leighton was poor, did you?"

Chapter 17

The Infamous Paper Route

Ricky, strangely enough, had always been ambitious, a bit of a "money-grubber," as I used to call him, and a hard worker. This seemed a contradiction of his carefree personality, but our dad made sure all of his boys understood what work was. Both my brother and I got our allowances every Saturday morning like clockwork from mom. But that ended for him when he acquired a Lethbridge Herald paper route at the age of nine; a job he hung onto for the next five years. I continued to get my weekly allowance in ever increasing increments as I got older much to Ricky's often-expressed consternation.

"What do you want me to do," I chirped back at him, "go to work for dad in the mill? Better yet, you could give me half your paper route." That usually ended the complaining.

119

He didn't actually mind the mundane routine involved in delivering the papers each day after school. After a bit he could probably have done it blindfolded. He couldn't stand anything that would upset the daily routines he had put into place to make his job easier. Then The Herald had the nerve, in his words, to request its paperboys provide their customers with receipts when they did their monthly collections.

"So, what's wrong with that?" I said. "It just makes sense to me."

"I've never had a single customer ever ask me for a receipt," Ricky replied indignantly.

"Well, as much as it bothers me to say this," I argued, "you're probably a better paper boy than a lot of the others out there. The Herald is probably just trying to keep everyone honest, maybe even some bad customers."

"I haven't had anyone not pay me, either," Ricky retorted, obviously feeling that he was losing ground with me. "Some even tip me every month. Do you think I want to stand out there in the freezing cold in the middle of winter writing out some stupid receipt for a customer who won't let me step in out of the cold? "Besides," he added to further advance his case, "I don't even know some of my customers' real names."

I snorted a laugh at that one, knowing that one of his regular customers was Pete the Painter and another Poor Charlie. Rather than bothering to find out their real names Ricky had also given his own nicknames to a few others like Old Johnny and my personal favorite, Log Cabin.

"Who the heck is Log Cabin?" I asked him one day when he mentioned it in passing.

"I don't know," he replied. "He's just this old bachelor guy who lives down by the swinging bridge in that old log shack with his dog Paddy."

"Oh, so you know his dog's name, but you don't know his? How can that be?"

"Well, he always calls his dog Paddy, but the dog doesn't say anything at all."

Something told me it was time to abandon this conversation.

Needless to say, the receipt book idea never really caught on with my brother, nor with any of the other Lethbridge Herald paperboys for that matter. The circulation department at the newspaper didn't seem to care that much as long as they received payment from the paperboys in accordance with their monthly billing.

Mom didn't pursue the matter either, other than to offer a mild suggestion that receipts wouldn't be a bad idea. After all, Ricky was nothing like his older brother, Walter, who may go down in the annals of paperboy history as one of the most irresponsible ever. Ricky had some financial smarts even at an early age. Walter didn't. Every month was the same. Walter would get his monthly bill from The Herald and not have enough from his collections to cover it, most of it having ended up in the till at Andy Oliva's confectionary downtown. Additionally, Walter had problems remembering who paid him each month and who didn't, so it was a regular occurrence to listen to our mom grilling him like a Gestapo commandant with a prisoner of war until she stomped away in shear frustration knowing that once again, she'd have to shell out to cover what he owed. Walter had a way of driving mom to absolute madness. Not because he wanted to. It was just the way he was.

One day I overheard her telling her friend, Louisa, who'd dropped by for coffee, that one of the happiest days of her life was when Walter finally gave up his paper route; a decision that had been made not without some urging.

To her relief Ricky was different. Two years into his paper route he'd already salted away over two hundred dollars and he used the money to buy Canada Savings Bonds. He took special delight in telling me, almost monthly, how much money he had in his bank account knowing full well that I didn't have an account at all. He could be so damned annoying.

He kept a record in his head of those paper customers who paid him and those who didn't, and the latter would get hounded daily until the money was forthcoming. On one occasion an old spinster who had been his customer since he took over the route paid Ricky with a paper bagful of pennies, 175 of them to be exact, or so it should have been. Ricky sat down on the step of her front porch and counted out the bag of coppers right then and there. The total came to 174. He recounted to make sure then knocked on the door and requested the extra penny.

"What did she do?" I asked Ricky, incredulous at his cheek and niggardliness.

"She laughed like crazy," he grinned. "Then she went into her kitchen, brought me a dime and stood there until I gave her back nine cents change."

I just couldn't help it. I sat on the edge of Ricky's bed and laughed until the tears ran down my face at the thought that she had given it back to him in equal measure.

That paper route was the seed of so much drama that often I would anxiously wait until after supper and make a point of asking Ricky what happened on the route that day as we were doing the supper dishes together. Mostly it was nothing, but on a few occasions there were some real gems.

Part of his route took him up the main street of town. One day he was confronted by Poor Charlie as he walked past the local GM dealership. Poor Charlie was anything but poor. He was one of the town's more prominent and prosperous business-men and owner of the said car dealership.

"He was standing out on the street talking to some guy when I was walking past," Ricky said. "He noticed me and asked me if I would sell him a newspaper. I told him I didn't have any spare ones to sell. He told me he'd give me 25 cents for one, which is 15 cents more than they sell for at the store. I told him again that I couldn't, because I really didn't have any extras.

"Then he looked at me and said, 'How about if I give you a dollar?'

"I'm ashamed to say that I was beginning to think of who of my regular customers wasn't going to get a paper that day. 'Okay,' I said, and was pulling a paper from my bag. He just let out a great big laugh, patted me on the top of his head, turned and walked back into his showroom."

Ricky, standing there with his dignity and his ethics now totally compromised, stomped in after him, determined to salvage something from this humiliation. Ten minutes later he walked out with a new, regular customer.

"What happened in the showroom?" I asked.

"Not much," he said. "I just walked into his office, dropped the paper on his desk and told him he'd be getting one delivered every day from then on, and that it would be $1.75 a month. He said he was already getting his Herald at home, and I told him I'd take care of that for him and that by having the paper delivered at work he wouldn't have to wait until he got home to catch up on the news of the day. Then he gave me another of his big laughs, opened the paper and began reading it right in front of me. As I was leaving his office he looked over the top of his paper and said, 'Hey kid, when you're old enough come back and see me. I can always use a good car salesman.'"

"So, who got shorted their newspaper, then?"

"No one," Ricky grinned. "I just went over to The Herald agent's place, told him Poor Charlie preferred getting his paper delivered at work and to cancel his home delivery. The agent gave me a spare paper to cover the shortage. He'll do that if you've got a good reason, but they watch really close for paperboys selling 'out of their bag' for spare cash.

"I can hardly wait to let Matt know that I've swiped one of his customers," my brother went on not even attempting to hide the glee on his face. "For the past year or so we've both had an even thirty customers each, and we've both been trying to get ahead of one another. Now I'm two up on him."

"But, you only took one of his customers," I said. "How do you get two out of that?"

"Simple," he replied, "I got one and he lost one.

Now I'm at thirty-one and he's at twenty-nine. Don't you get it?"

That's just how my brother's brain worked, and I couldn't understand for the life of me why it had taken him almost the entire year in Grade Four to memorize his times tables.

"I can't figure you out, Ricky. Matt's definitely your best friend. How can you do something like that to someone who's your best friend? If I did that to Marlene she'd likely never forgive me, and I wouldn't blame her."

"You'll probably never understand it, Katty," he said. "We do it because we're best friends. I fully expect him to get even with me somewhere down the road."

He was right… totally beyond my comprehension.

"Mrs. Anderson lives with old Sam Tymchuk," Ricky informed me one day, just out of the blue.

"Well now, that's terribly interesting," I replied in my most derisive manner. "Who's Mrs. Anderson, and even more importantly, who's old Sam Tymchuk?"

"They're paper customers of mine," Ricky replied, once again seeming to ignore my mockery. "They have different last names, but I'm sure they're together, you know, like mom and dad are. Married."

"So," I said, "you've got one customer you call Old Johnny because you can't bother to find out his last name, and you have another that's two different people with two different last names and you know them both. Go figure. This may come as a shock to you, brother, but people do live together without being married."

"Don't be such a snip," he shot back at me, an edge of irritation in his voice. "It's just that I spend more time with Sam and Mrs. Anderson than with my other customers. On really cold winter days they let me come in and she makes me a big cup of cocoa. Sam's out in the yard a lot, so I usually stop and chat with him for a while, almost every day, actually. He's the one who told me cats always land on their feet no matter what. He even let me test that out with his own cat, Muggins, and he's right. Muggins wasn't too impressed, though, and took off after the second time I dropped her."

I could do nothing but give Ricky my trademark big sister eye roll; something I found myself doing more often these days. If nothing else, my brother was learning a few things about life.

"Sam's pretty smart, too," he continued. "The other day he was out back of his yard sawing up logs for winter firewood with a big old crosscut saw and the sweat was pouring off him. He stopped when I came by and we talked a bit. I asked him why he was still using wood when almost everyone in town had converted to natural gas.

"'Well, you know, Ricky,' he said, 'Wood's better than gas because it heats you twice—once when you're cutting it up and again when you put it in the stove.'

"Can't argue with that," I conceded, reflecting on its notable wisdom.

The Paperboy Chronicles, as I came to affectionately refer to them, weren't always about Ricky per se, but they invariably made me chuckle.

Over supper dishes one evening Ricky laughingly related a story Matt had told him. Like Ricky, Matt Mitchell had a real offbeat sense of humor, made more amusing by his appearance. A shock of out-of-control curly hair sat atop a face that conveyed a comic earnestness.

As he was delivering the papers one afternoon he stopped to take a break and sat down on the front steps of Mrs. Costello's house after he'd dropped the paper in her mailbox.

"While he was sitting there a salesman-looking guy came through the gate, approached Matt and asked him if his mother was home," Ricky related. "Matt told him that she was at work. Almost at the same time Mrs. Costello came to the door to fetch the paper Matt had just delivered. 'I thought you said your mother wasn't home?' the fellow said. 'She isn't,' Matt replied. 'I don't live here.'"

Hearing this, I couldn't restrain a giggle, but knowing Matt as I did I wasn't sure whether he was trying to be funny or just making humor out of his own idiocy. You couldn't tell with those guys sometimes.

Chapter 18

Snakes and Ladders

Why is it that in any group of boys a hierarchy invariably forms? Maybe that's just how we humans function, but among boys there is no subtlety about it at all. Their respective roles in the pecking order couldn't be more defined if they all wore badges. The two most obvious positions are the leader and, sadly to say, the whipping boy. The latter is the one who bears the brunt of the cruelty that is inherent in nearly every group of young boys.

There are no immediately identifiable markers that define the whipping boy. He's often not the worst looking of the group, nor the most awkward or stupid. What he invariably does have is an obsessional need to be part of the group, combined with the inability to disguise that need. Whipping boys take their lumps and keep coming back for more. Even more strangely, they are never ejected from their group, because on some level that group needs them as well and for a whole range of reasons.

Well, enough of the psychobabble for one day. In Ricky's group the unenviable position of whipping boy went to Perry Edwards. Most of the crap he had to put up with from the little band of thugs was pretty low level; the presumed damage to his self-esteem tenuously balanced by the continued acceptance by his peers.

Appearance-wise, Perry could best be described as pablum; straight, brownish hair, brown eyes, medium height and build, and with an ever so slight stoop when he walked, that being his single distinguishing characteristic. In school he was a straight A student, so he did not lack intelligence.

Marlene and I were coming from downtown after browsing through the new arrivals in the girls' wear department at Thompson's Store after school. We were kind of glad to look over the new stuff without our moms there to tell us what was darling and pretty and making us go into the dressing room to try on some hideous outfit that we absolutely despised.

Anyway, we were crossing over the tracks on the way home near where the town's public works building is and across the street from where the Lethbridge Herald delivery van dropped off the bundles of papers every day for the local paperboys, one of whom was my brother.

From the tracks, a distance of about a block, we could see and hear someone on top of a sixteen-foot, rickety-looking, old wooden ladder, right in the middle of the street. The poor guy was screaming in terror as the ladder wavered back and forth like a tree in the wind. At the bottom were four or five guys, my brother included, holding the ladder in its upright position.

"Is that guy at the top... is that Perry Edwards?" Marlene remarked with undisguised alarm.

It was Perry, all right, sixteen feet in the air. His arms and legs were tethered to the ladder, like Jesus on the cross, tied there with discarded twine used to wrap the delivered newspaper bundles.

In panic, Marlene and I ran over screaming at the boys and pretty much ordering them to lower the ladder very carefully and to untie Perry. Ricky and his henchmen were all smiling, until they saw the look on my face.

I don't curse that often, but I couldn't hold it back this time, I feared so much for Perry. "What the fuck do you guys think you're doing?" I spat out. The smile was off the faces of every one of them as they stood there not quite knowing what to do next and obviously shocked at the language coming out of my mouth.

"Lower him down... now!" I ordered. "We'll help you, and don't you guys dare let it go."

Marlene and I helped them lower the ladder just to make sure they didn't drop it. Perry had been in tears. You could tell from the streaks down his face, but once the ladder was lying flat on the ground and the boys began untying him, I could not help but notice that stupid smile of bravado that came over his face. As he got to his feet he said to the guys, "What a view!" as though he'd climbed up there himself to take a look.

"What the hell are you smiling at, you stupid ass?" I screamed. "Two minutes ago you were up there crying like a baby. Now you're acting like some big shot."

Just as I was giving him a thorough tongue-lashing, Marlene stepped in and before anyone knew it she hauled off and punched Perry squarely on the nose. Blood squirted out everywhere, and Marlene just turned around and walked away.

I caught up to her quickly and said, "Why did you do that?"

"Because you didn't," she replied.

Now I knew for sure why she was my best friend. There were times when I wished I could be more like her, but I knew I never would. I was glad she was by my side, ditzy as she might be sometimes, to be the me I couldn't be on my own.

Bored while waiting for the papers to arrive, the guys had apparently found the old wooden ladder stored up against the side of the Town Shop. They grabbed Perry and some twine from the garbage barrel and tied him securely to the narrow end of the ladder.

"Perry thought it was funny at first," Ricky told me later, "until we managed to get the ladder completely upright."

That's when the terror set in at the knowledge he was sixteen feet up there helplessly tied and at the mercy of five guys who might not have the strength to keep him there. One little mistake and he could drop face first, onto the pavement.

"Actually, I was a little worried myself," Ricky admitted. "We were kind of scared to even start letting the ladder down just in case we couldn't hold onto it. Perry could have really been hurt. I guess it was kind of stupid of us."

"Yeah, stupid... just like you," I said curtly, still angry and in disbelief at the whole spectacle, including Perry's bloodied nose.

I really wanted to report this one to mom and dad at supper. Ricky really deserved a good bawling out from dad and an accompanying guilt trip from mom. Then I remembered that insipid smile on Perry's face and decided to let it go. There are some things in life you can't change, others that aren't worth the effort.

Chapter 19

A Little Sociological Perspective

I know I'm well into this journal, but now might be a good time to put Ricky and his peccadillos aside for a moment and talk briefly about Blairmore in particular, and the Crowsnest Pass in general.

I'll start by saying that The Crowsnest Pass is a community like none other.

You might counter, "Well, I grew up in a small town, too, and there were other small towns just like ours down the road a bit. So I can identify."

Nope. Sorry, not the same. Anyone who has lived in The Pass or visited, even for a short time, knows exactly what I'm talking about. What's peculiar is that those who were born, raised and stayed in The Pass are the ones that don't recognize its inherent differentness. That's to be expected, since they have little basis for comparison.

The area is unique not simply because of its geography, though that plays an important role, but because of countless factors that have gone into weaving its very fabric.

A newspaper journalist who once visited the area at the height of its coal mining days described his impression of The Pass as "a grimy string of pearls" referring to the dirty, coal dust encrusted small towns and villages strung along Highway 3 and the CPR rail line from Bellevue on the east to Coleman on the west.

Presumably, his reference to pearls under that obvious layer of coal dust would indicate that he had made the effort to identify the strange and palpably unique quality of the area and its people. And, had he taken the time to drive or hike even half a mile north or south of the highway he would have discovered, doubtlessly to his surprise, a pristine wilderness that was the playground of the locals, both young and old. Coal mining had, for certain, left its share of scars but on otherwise natural and unblemished beauty.

Though the Crowsnest Pass geographically

straddled the boundary between Alberta and British Columbia it was generally conceded that, when referring to it in any way other than strictly geographical terms, Crowsnest Pass was solely the purview of five distinct communities: Bellevue, Hillcrest, Frank, Blairmore and Coleman, all on the very western and most southerly edge of Alberta. And for good reason, it seems. In those heady days when coal was king, the residents on the Alberta side had little but contempt for their neighbors on the B.C. side. This, in spite of the fact that even then a great number of miners travelled daily to work in the coal mines there.

The ill feelings were, to be sure, reciprocal. But it was the Alberta side that, with time worn tradition, appropriated the mantle of being The Crowsnest Pass. Their B.C. neighbors to the west, Michel and Natal, were filthy little hovels with few redeeming qualities other than being within walking distance to the nearby underground mines that kept them in groceries and the other necessities of life.

Though united in their disrespect for their B.C. neighbors, a watered-down version of that very same disposition existed between the five Pass communities... well, perhaps not so "watered down".

Since every one of the five grew up around its own coal mine, or mines, and since transportation in the early days was limited, each town had a sense of its own independence, and importance. The result was three towns and two villages, each with its own municipal government, its own schools, playgrounds and parks, arena, fire and public works department, post office and business sector. For many, many years, when coal powered industry and the railways, and heated practically every home in the country, each of these communities prospered and grew. The irony that there existed five completely separate, autonomous towns, stretched along less than twelve miles of highway, scarcely raised an eyebrow of concern.

The Pass was a nemesis for the travelling public as well. With the exception of Hillcrest, the highway ran right through the center of each town accompanied by the requisite twenty-five mile per hour speed limit. It took nearly as long to travel from the west end of Coleman to the east end of Bellevue as it did to travel the additional thirty-five miles to the next major town, Pincher Creek, the latter leg of the trip unencumbered by any municipal speed limits.

All of this incongruity was to change with the fortunes of the coal industry—but that's another story for a different time.

The competitive nature and jealousies that existed between the five communities was further exacerbated through sports. Whether it was hockey in winter or baseball in summer each town raised its own teams, and they competed fiercely with each other. This competitiveness spilled out of the valley on the rare occasion when games could be arranged with communities outside of the cloistered confines of the Pass. The net result, doubtlessly well earned, was a reputation for tough, nasty, almost unsportsmanlike combativeness. That, over time, became a defining perception, if not characteristic, of the Pass in general. Little to nothing was done to discourage this notion.

If Canada defined itself as the melting pot of the world, then the Crowsnest Pass was a complete and unaltered microcosm of that. To meet the heavy labor requirements of the coal mining industry generations of immigrants arrived in the Pass from virtually every corner of the world, with the vast majority from Western and Eastern Europe.

The concentration of all of these nationalities

141

and cultures in the tight semi-isolation of a mountain pass community was perhaps the single influence that gave the Crowsnest Pass its unique ethnic and cultural flavor. No single group was large enough to be dominant and the area was simply too small for any to form significant ethnic neighborhoods, though that was not entirely true. Ricky and I had friends from at least a dozen different nationalities. Our neighborhood, though of mixed heritage, was predominantly Italian. Consequently then, they constituted the majority of our friends.

What was different, you might ask?

Not a single thought seemed ever given over to any form of prejudice in all the years that I was growing up—not ethnic, not religious, and not (as they like to say these days) socio-economic. That realization didn't strike me until late in my teen years when Social Studies classes tweaked an interest in such matters and I realized the anomaly that was the town in which we lived. If we despised anyone and I use this term facetiously it was those damned kids from Coleman (or Bellevue, or Hillcrest). We could tolerate those kids from Frank. After all, it was merely a stone's throw away and practically a suburb of Blairmore.

This was where the Callaghan family landed in the summer of 1952.

If you hailed from the prairies to the east, the likelihood was that you came from towns where you could see an equal distance in all directions, and you could go somewhere without actually having to cross over a creek or river, a railway track or a highway. In the Crowsnest Pass the sun rose and set at markedly different times depending on which of the five towns you lived in, or for that matter, in which part of town your house happened to be located. People could grow stuff in their gardens in Hillcrest, for example, that was impossible to grow in Blairmore, not because of soil conditions, but because Hillcrest got that precious extra hour or so of morning sun by virtue of the fact that it was on the east end of the valley.

But this is not a historical treatise, and I shall make no claims with regard to the veracity in the characterization of my hometown. I'm certain there are those who might consider my opinions shallow and incompetent, but this is my journal and mine alone. Should it fall upon contrarian eyes I make no apology for my observations.

Chapter 20

The Big One That Got Away

Here we go again. Ricky's once more found himself in a whole heap of trouble with mom and dad. I'm not sure whether he's soft in the head, or possessed of such unshakeable conviction in his own infallibility that it overpowers the scintilla of common sense he does have. Add that to his laudable powers of persuasion and you've got a real formula for trouble.

My brother didn't have to tell me about this one. I was there when it happened and took in the whole mindless affair. I suppose it was unavoidable, after all. A perfect storm, if you will, of ripening adolescence, its accompanying irresponsibility and that secret ingredient ever present in such situations—opportunity.

It was always a rule in our house that during the school year Sunday evenings were reserved for homework, after which, if completed we were allowed to watch The Ed Sullivan Show or Bonanza. So, we were homebound and going out for any reason other than a scheduled event was not an option.

Around 7 o'clock, Ricky's buddy Nick came to the door looking for my brother. Ricky went to the door and let him know that he couldn't go out. It was something his friend should have already known.

Nick, it seemed, had swiped a bottle of beer from his dad's stash and invited Ricky out to the old abandoned neighbor's shed in the back alley to drink it with him. Regretfully, my brother couldn't join him, but came up with what I will call Plan B. Don't ask me why this makes any sense, but here was the plan, as Ricky related to me after his dressing down from our parents.

First of all, we mustn't confuse this with being any sort of social get together. Nick was to go back out to the alley and drink his half of the beer. When he was done he was to bring the bottle to the side of the house, right under Ricky's bedroom dormer window. Unfortunately, that window was right above the big picture window in the living room, but Ricky had the solution to that problem, too.

Shortly before going back upstairs he walked casually into the living room and closed the drapes on the picture window (something, I might add here, that he had never done before in his entire life). Sitting there watching T.V., both mom and dad thought the whole thing a little suspicious. It was still daylight outside. They promptly reopened the drapes when Ricky left the room.

Now this is the part of the story that is both a testament to Ricky's audacity and persuasive powers. The plan was that Ricky would use his fishing rod to drop the line down to Nick from his open bedroom window. Nick would then tie the bottle of beer to the end of the fishing line and Ricky would reel it back up to his window. Simple. Effective. Foolproof. Right?

As Nick crouched under the sill of the living room window he yelled as quietly as possible up to Ricky that the living room drapes were, in fact, open. Ricky called back down that this was impossible since he had just closed them. This went back and forth with a few more exchanges before Nick finally relented, tied the beer to the fishing line, said his goodbyes and hightailed it back home. Both mom and dad looked out the picture window in amazement as a bottle of beer ascended jerkily in front of their eyes, seemingly floating on its own since the fishing line was invisible to them.

It didn't take them more than a few seconds to figure it out, though. My brother no sooner had the beer in his window before mom yelled upstairs for him to come down, "right now, and bring that beer bottle with you." Lounging in my bedroom and reading with my door closed, this was the only part of the exchange that I heard, other than the subsequent yelling when Ricky obeyed the order and took the beer down to the kitchen where mom and dad were waiting.

To his credit, my brother disavowed my involvement or any knowledge in the matter, so that night I got to watch "Bonanza." Ricky didn't—for the next six weeks. That was accompanied by a concurrent six weeks of grounding, which ultimately ended up being less than four since Ricky's constant and annoying presence in the house was doubtlessly tougher on mom than it was on him.

Though our parents suspected it was Nick involved at the other end in the beer debacle, due to his earlier visit that evening, Ricky refused to, "rat him out" (his words). Lacking any rock solid evidence the matter was quietly dropped.

Perhaps it's because I had fewer friends and was never really up to mischief, but I always felt that on some level our parents, and particularly our dad, held a begrudging respect for the bond of silence that was some sort of honor code with Ricky and his lot of close friends. I can honestly say that I cannot recall a single time when any of them got into trouble because one of them tattled or squealed on the others. They'd do the Cosa Nostra proud.

Nick's dad and ours' were friends and business associates, so I suspect that in the course of things they compared notes and probably had a great laugh—to themselves, of course—over the whole episode. Boys will be boys, so they say, and that's probably because dads will be dads.

When I went back upstairs after Bonanza, Ricky was licking the side of this plastic rechargeable flashlight that he had gotten as a paperboy Christmas bonus from The Herald. "This thing tastes weird," he said, handing it to me.

I could immediately see that white, powdery battery acid had leaked through one of the cracks in the side of the light, probably due to my brother forgetting and leaving it plugged into the wall for two weeks. "You're such a fool," I said, taking the flashlight gingerly between two fingernails and depositing it in the garbage downstairs.

I'm sure he thought I was talking about the flashlight, but really I was referring to the beer matter. It was always confusing on those occasions when I had to chastise him for more than one thing at a time.

Chapter 21

Not Exactly a Great Vintage

Ricky's tent, the cheap, teepee-style one with no floor and the tacky Indian Chief Head decal imprinted over its door flap, had mysteriously gone missing. Naturally, because our parents had a pretty good handle on our family possessions, the question of where the tent had, in the favorite words of our mother, "taken wings to" came up. In a makeshift attempt to buy him enough time to conjure up a believable reason for its absence Ricky volunteered to mount a search for the tent, with assurances that it just had to be in the house somewhere.

Something told me this was going to be another one of his doozies and I could hardly wait to put him to my own interrogation knowing that it would unearth the truth. It turned out to be more of a tale than I was prepared for.

"Remember when us guys were playing around the old mine site a couple of weeks ago?" Ricky reminded me as though I was just expected to keep a running tab of his comings and goings.

"Yes," I lied.

"Well, we were in one of those old mine shacks," he said, "and under the bench, tucked behind some old burlap sacking, Karl spotted a dirty old gallon bottle, three-quarters full of this thick dark red stuff. We thought it was oil or something, but when we unscrewed the cap and smelled it, we knew it was definitely wine."

I nodded and patiently waited with a mounting degree of dread for the rest of the story. Over the years I had learned to be patient when Ricky related his misadventures knowing from experience that the further back from the story's outcome he started, the worse the story was going to be. Besides, it would be like reading the last chapter of a novel then going back and reading the rest of it from the beginning. Anyway, I did take some solace in the knowledge that my brother was still sitting in front of me relating the story rather than staring lifelessly up at us from a gurney.

"So you guys took it down to the river, set it up

and threw rocks at it until it broke and spilled all that crap into the water," I volunteered, knowing with some certainty that I was probably way off base since that scenario bore no relationship whatsoever to the missing tent. But hope, as you know, springs eternal.

"No," confirmed my brother. "We took it over to Karl's place and he grabbed one of his mother's pillow cases and we strained the stuff into a pot, washed out the jug real good and poured the stuff back in. We couldn't get the red stains out of the pillowcase, so we had to throw it away. When we were straining it out there was all this sludgy stuff in the bottom of the jug, so we ended up with just a little over half a gallon by the time we were done."

As usual, I waited for the rest of the tale to unfold with my typical mixture of dread and fascination.

"We decided that the best plan would be to have an overnight campout up at The Flats," said Ricky. "Just the five of us: Nick, Karl, Matt, Stevie and me."

"No sleeping bags?" I asked.

"Nope," he said. "Just us and my teepee tent.

And that jug of whatever it was. Then my tent got knocked over and fell right into our bonfire and the top got completely burned off before we could rescue it. We had to get rid of it."

"Well, there you go again," I shot back, "skipping right over a few important chapters. The whole story, please."

"It was really a bad night," Ricky finally admitted. "There's a lot of it that I just can't remember. We set the tent up, built the fire and then started in on the jug of that disgusting tasting brew, along with a big old White Owl stogie that Nick had brought along for the occasion. It was fun for a bit. The stuff really tasted awful, but none of us wanted to chicken out and be the first to pass on our turn.

"But, things started to get a little crazy after passing the jug around a few times. Stevie and Matt were puking sick from smoking that cigar. Karl was acting really crazy, running around, swinging that hatchet, howling like a wolf and yelling something in Polish. Then he fell down on my tent and knocked it over on to the bonfire. We couldn't get him off the tent fast enough and that's when the top of it burned off.

"After that, everything sort of became a blur until we woke up the next morning. Karl was gone. Where, we didn't know. The fire had gone out and the entire top of my tent was destroyed. The four of us who were still there were deathly sick and didn't dare go home in that condition, so we stayed there for most of the day recovering. All of us eventually had to take a shit, so we ripped off pieces from the damaged tent to wipe our ass with. Better than leaves, I guess."

I knew this story was going to be a bad one, but the collective stupidity of these five had me absolutely dumbfounded.

"Do you have any fucking idea how completely insane that was," I screeched, realizing instantly that I used the "f" word out loud. Ricky shot me a look of absolute shock, both at my outburst and my use of the invective. "You guys could have all been poisoned. You had no idea what was in that jug, other than the fact that is smelled like wine. What a great news story that would have made, I railed on: 'Five local boys found poisoned to death.'"

Tears welled up in my eyes, and for the first time ever, the look on my brother's face told me that he regretted his confession to me. The brother/sister bond that we had forged seemed about to break, sadly, as the forces of love, caring and compassion collided head on with recklessness and thoughtless disregard. I knew I had to save it. Sobbing uncontrollably, I hugged my brother soaking the shoulder of his shirt with my tears.

"I love you," I said in his ear. "Why do you keep doing this to me?"

He just stood there, his arms limply at his side. I know he wanted to push me away, but he didn't dare. For me, there would be time later to preach caution but not tonight. There would be time to deal with the strange foreboding that haunted me always, but not tonight.

After a requisite day or so Ricky confessed to our mother that he had accidently burned a hole in the tent when it blew over in the wind and toppled into the bonfire. That was the entirety of the story. After a scolding from her for being careless and lying to her about it, the matter, again, was quietly dropped.

Chapter 22

The Problem with Early Wealth

I often had to go to mom for money if I wanted anything extra or special (before I got that job as usher at the Orpheum Theatre when I was fifteen) but the same couldn't be said for Ricky, or for that matter, most of his friends. They all seemed to have money, because from very early ages they all had jobs. Menial as they may have been the net result was that all the guys had been pretty much weaned off their childhood allowances by the age of ten or so and they always seemed to have cash in their pockets.

Truthfully, I found it just a bit irksome that they all loaned money back and forth between each other with little regard, but Heaven forbid that I should ever chance to borrow a dollar from my brother. He'd want to know what I needed it for, when he could expect it back, and on and on and on. After a few episodes of that I just gave it up and went without. Brothers can be such a pain in the ass. But here I was, once again, looking for the why in his behavior. I came to the conclusion that, unlike his friends, I may not have had the where-withal to repay any debt I incurred with him and therefore, sister or not, I was a credit risk.

But, that's not really where I was headed with this chapter of my journal. As flush as they were, they were all constantly on the lookout for other money making opportunities, including this little gem.

Ricky, Nick, and two other friends hitchhiked to Coleman one afternoon with the express belief that they just might be allowed into Downtown Billiards and Snooker. Like Johnny's in Bellevue, it was as seedy a pool hall dive as you would expect any depression era carryover to be. There was a certain incongruity about those old-school pool halls. To the last one they were all drafty, poorly lit and inadequately heated dumps. The furnishings, however, were without exception spectacular, from the gigantic six by twelve foot slate pool tables themselves to the opulent counters, well-worn benches and cue racks; all hand-carved quarter-cut oak; deep, rich, real, and without exception, out-dated.

You had to be sixteen to legally get into any pool hall, a fact that Ricky and his three companions were amply aware of from previous unsuccessful efforts in their hometown. They'd heard, though, that if Sal was on shift at the Coleman joint, he'd often bend the rules a bit and turn a blind eye, especially in the afternoons when the cops seldom bothered to do any checking.

Getting into a pool hall back then was the Golden Fleece of accomplishment for all boys considered minors, and pulling it off, no matter where, could result in serious bragging rights, not to mention the accompanying spike in status. So off they went, all four of them in one pack, thumbing it the three miles from Blairmore to Coleman.

Sal, the crusty old pool hall owner, immediately identifiable by the cigarette dangling loosely from the side of his mouth, took one disinterested look at them from over the counter. In a weary effort to at least provide them with some exiting dignity he requested they produce their I.D.s, and in keeping with the charade, each of the nervous foursome fumbled in his pockets for non-existent wallets and collectively admitted, in a last ditch effort

158

at face saving, that they had all inadvertently left them at home.

Through a haze of cigarette smoke drifting lazily up into his eyes, Sal flashed a brief smirk and the boys got the message as his squinting eyes shifted off them and to the front door. Then the boys noticed the briefest of hesitations as they prepared their chastened departure. Then, a glimmer of hope. Never one to pass on an opportunity to make an extra buck or two, particularly on a slow, lazy Saturday afternoon, Sal asked the boys if they'd ever bowled before. Nick was the only one to nod in the affirmative while the others just stood in silence wondering what was coming next. Sal nodded again, this time toward a small, two-lane five-pin bowling alley on the far side of the pool hall which none of the four had even noticed when they came in.

"There's no age restrictions there," he confided in a conspiratorial tone that appealed to the boys. Considering it at least a partial victory, all four agreed to give bowling a shot and shelled out a buck apiece while Sal shrewdly figured out how to sweeten the deal. If they agreed to set up their own pins, he offered, they could play two games for the price of one.

The guys were really starting to like Coleman. Ricky and Nick volunteered to be the pinsetters, which meant that they had to run down the edge of the lane each time the knocked down pins needed to be moved or set back up. Nearly two hours later, with the bowling balls spending the greater part of their time in the gutters, the game wrapped up with no real winner since keeping score wasn't one of the skills Nick had picked up in his earlier bowling experience.

Sal didn't seem to mind. At one point he even left the boys on their own while he went out to have a quick mid-afternoon beer or two at the hotel bar up the street. Ricky and Nick seized the opportunity to grab a tray of snooker balls from behind Sal's counter and make a few shots on one of the big billiard tables before he returned; a small victory that guaranteed huge boasting rights.

On their way out the door Sal called Ricky and Nick back to the counter. They looked at each other with a sense of dread. Had Sal somehow figured out that they'd played some pool in his absence? Were they about to be banned for life from ever darkening the doors of his pool hall? Neither, as it turned out.

Complimenting them on the great job at setting their own pins Sal asked if they wanted to come back later that day and be the pin setters for the evening crowd, since his regular guys were going to be unavailable that night. Assuring them that Saturday nights were always very busy, and offering them twenty-five cents each per game, the chance of making big money was simply irresistible to the two go-getters. They'd be back at seven.

And they were. After a briefing from Sal which included the cautionary note that they were, at all times, to keep their eyes open while setting up the pins and putting the balls in the ball return lane.

"Never take your eyes off the bowlers," he cautioned. "You could get hurt."

He explained to the two novices that for some bowlers, particularly those that had a few beers in them, the real sport was not getting strikes or spares, but seeing if they could hit the pinsetters when they weren't paying attention.

"Oh, nice," Nick replied. "So what you're telling us is that we're actually the targets."

"Some nights," Sal admitted.

For two hours Ricky and Nick sat on their

perches above the backstops, those heavy tan colored leather bags filled with sand and suspended just behind the pins. And for two infinitely boring hours neither of them made a nickel. They spent the first half hour honing their pin setting speed and skill. Time well spent they were soon to find out. At just around nine a rowdy crowd of drunken 20-somethings came in and the boredom soon turned to terror.

Ricky related to me how they were, for sure, in very real danger and the briefing they'd received from Sal barely scratched the surface.

"Some of those guys could throw a ball down the alley as fast as a bullet," he said. "Others would loft the ball and you wouldn't know it was coming until it hit the floor with a loud bang halfway down the alley. You couldn't take your eyes off the bowlers for a second, but you were expected to set the pins up perfectly in their V-formation. Some of the balls hit the leather backstop so hard that the perch we had to sit on would shake like crazy."

The "Night of Terror," as I delighted in calling it, ended at just after midnight. For the whole night, Nick took home a dollar and Ricky pocketed seventy-five cents. Sal didn't even bat an eye as he handed the boys their earnings, all in quarters.

"I think from the looks on our faces, Sal could pretty much tell that we were his new crew of 'regular guys', and like the ones we'd just replaced, certain not to show up for next Saturday night's shift," Ricky said.

But, the night wasn't quite over yet. It had been easy to hitchhike a ride to Coleman in the early evening. Kids hitch-hiking between the towns in the Pass was a common practice, and it was a "real asshole", as Ricky liked to say, who wouldn't pick up local youngsters thumbing rides between the towns. But it was quite a different story going home after midnight. Other than transport trucks, which didn't pick up hitchhikers, there was virtually no traffic. Ricky and Nick didn't get home until nearly two a.m. having hoofed it the entire way. Mom and dad were up, worried sick and about to call the police. In their wisdom neither Ricky nor Nick had bothered to tell their parents their plans for the evening.

The raised voices downstairs woke me from a dead sleep. After what seemed like an eternity Ricky came stomping upstairs. I opened my bedroom door as he reached the top, his eyes glued to the floor, and I quietly asked him what had happened.

"Nothing," he growled back to me, then as a second thought added, "I'll tell you in the morning." And with that dumb-assed, quirky little smile that had long ago endeared him to me he finished with, "Cuz it doesn't look like I'll be going anywhere any time soon."

"Hmm... grounded again, eh?" I correctly surmised.

Chapter 23

Four for a Penny

Good Lord, my soul for a thesaurus. I find myself in desperate want of synonyms for stupidity in order that this journal does not become too repetitive. My fault, I guess, for thinking that I could diarize the peccadillos of my brother and his ilk while maintaining some pretense of literary competence. Please allow me some preamble here to put actions into some sort of context.

Down on the east end of Blairmore's main street is Andy Oliva's Confectionery. I will use the term confectionery simply for lack of a better term to describe it. Convenience store would give Andy's place grandiosity somewhat akin to comparing a country church to St. Peter's Basilica. Confectionery would indicate its offerings were limited solely to candy and the like which also isn't that exacting, since Andy sold other necessities such as cigarettes, cigars, snuff, plug tobacco and pop. I throw pop in there simply to make it clear that he could scarcely be considered a tobacconist, either. My recollections of his exact inventories are clouded less by poor memory than by the fact that most of us kids were there simply for the candy. Little else really captured our attention.

At any rate Andy managed to forge out for himself a very fine living, largely on the nickels, dimes and quarters passed over his counter by kids in exchange for what was known in the day as penny candy; carefully hand counted and doled out in small, brown paper bags. "Hand counted?" you might ask, thinking me possibly a bit pretentious in my description of a rather mundane act. The truth is quite the opposite.

Andy's wares: jujubes, jawbreakers, flavored wax lips and moustaches, licorice whips, gumballs, niggerbabies and much, much more, were all displayed in their open topped cardboard boxes beneath a glass-topped counter. The runaway favorite of most of the boys in the neighborhood was arrows, which were nothing more than jujubes formed in the shape of an arrow, and in an assorted range of five or six colors. Unlike the jujubes that sat in a box right next to them, arrows were four for a penny while the jujubes themselves were three for a penny. An obvious value advantage, right? The boys thought so, likely because it took roughly the same amount of time to glom down ten cents worth of arrows as it did the more expensive jujubes.

Allow me to describe here a typical transaction carried on with such frequency that a small area of the glass countertop was no longer clear glass, but worn over time to a hazy translucence. Ricky, or one of his buddies, would put their money on the counter and ask Andy for a dime's worth of arrows. Andy would reach into the box and grab a full handful, drop them all on the countertop and count out forty. He'd sweep the overage back in the box, grab one of his small brown paper bags, scoop up the candy and put it in the bag. If one fell on the floor he would pick it up and put it in the bag with the rest. God help you if you even complained about that. I'm not saying that it never happened, but I personally can't recall Andy wiping off the counter unless someone had ordered those yucky fake strawberry candies with the sugary coating. Then he'd have to sweep the loose sugar off the counter onto the floor with his hand.

Given that he dealt largely in sugar, I'm pretty certain that he did do a wipe-down at least once at the end of the day.

Andy himself was a big man, or so he seemed to us as young kids. He had been a semi-professional boxer in his younger days and it showed in his broad chest and shoulders, though he'd managed to put on a pound or two in other areas as well. His hands were large with fingers resembling those jointed bulk wieners you see at meat counters. When he grabbed a mitt full of candy it was always at least fifty cents worth even at four for a penny. You could be sure that every candy, in every box under Andy's counter, was handled by him ten or more times. You could also be sure that any landing accidentally on the floor never found their way into his garbage can.

But that's the way things were back then. I recall going to Landry's Meat Market with mom. The pork chops looked good, so she asked for half a dozen. When Mr. Landry was packaging them up one fell on the floor. He picked it up, scraped off the sawdust with his boning knife and put it in with the other five.

The butcher just smiled over the counter at mom and me and said, "That chop's probably been in worse places than that."

"Someday I'm going to stop dealing here, Harold," my mom replied. She never did. They were friends.

Anyway, back to Oliva's.

For a lot of the kids, mostly boys, between the ages of eight and fourteen, Andy's was somewhat of a hangout. The guys in Ricky's pack of friends seldom went there solo but in groups of two or more. There was a limit since Andy's store was so tiny that eight customers at a time constituted a crushing crowd. Whether waiting for the theatre up the street to open its doors or for another friend to arrive, hours were spent hanging around Oliva's dingy little place. Andy didn't seem to mind much either since it usually translated into more sales for him.

Loitering had its downside though, as Ricky divulged to me one afternoon as we lounged around on the back lawn under the lilac bushes that were mom's pride and joy, and were later proved to be the chief culprits in Ricky's annual springtime allergy attacks.

"Did you hear what happened to Nick last

week at Oliva's?" he asked me, as if it was information that may have already swept through the
entire community like a tornado of gossip and in-
nuendo. It wasn't as though that didn't happen in
a community like ours where tragedies and other
serious misfortunes occurred with some degree of
regularity.

"No," I replied, "but I'm certain that I'm
about to. Should we be whispering?" I could often
not resist sarcasm as an almost involuntary response to my brother's confidences, no doubt because it allowed me the necessary time to put myself in a proper state of mind. Sadly, for me, good
sarcasm always seemed wasted on Ricky.

"We were hanging around Oliva's waiting for
the Orpheum to open for the Saturday matinee,"
he went on, "me, Nick, Stevie and Matt. We'd all
bought some candy and were just waiting for a few
of the other guys to show up. Nick was standing
over by the ice cream fridge and Andy just stepped
out from behind the counter, walked up to him and
asked him what he had in his jacket pocket. Nick
kind of looked dumbly at him and didn't say anything, but Andy just stood there waiting. Nick
reached into his pocket and pulled out a Fudgesicle
that he'd taken from the freezer and sheepishly

handed it over. When he did, Andy took it with one hand then slapped Nick squarely across the face with the other. Christ, you could hear the slap through the whole store and it practically knocked Nick off his feet. Andy used to be a boxer, y'know."

I couldn't resist a smile as I visualized the whole thing, since Nick had never been one of my favorites. Being that he was one of Ricky's closest buddies, I'd frequently found myself begrudgingly making allowances for his bad behavior. "So, then what happened?" I asked, possibly too eagerly, my curiosity piqued and in conflict with my practiced aloofness.

"Well, that was the real weird part," said Ricky, with a sort of quizzical look on his face. "Nothing happened. Andy just put the Fudgesicle back in the fridge, walked back around the counter and that was that. Nothing more was said at all."

"You mean he never kicked Nick out of the store; didn't even ban him from coming back in, not even for a week?" I asked now equally incredulous.

"Nope. Nothing. Nick didn't even walk out himself voluntarily. I know I would have," said Ricky. "I think Andy believed the slap was enough. I know Nick did," he added with a quick smile. "The red mark was still on his face when we came out of the theatre after the matinee. I'm pretty sure he won't try shoplifting at Andy's anymore. Nor will the rest of us."

As I lay on my bed that night the scenario played out vividly in my mind. I seldom give little more than a passing thought to most of my brother's wayward tales, particularly those that involve his delinquent friends. I thought less about Nick than I did about Andy, the latter's judicious and appropriate application of punishment and discipline, the whole idea of the entire community taking a part in the raising of its children. These were heady thoughts for a girl barely fifteen, but I think that I understood. I understood that community isn't a place. It's not a city or a town, not even a neighborhood. It's a way of being, of how people live together in those physical spaces.

On a much lighter note, I must relate yet another incident that took place at that little confectionery that was so much a part of my brother's daily life. With little else to talk about, Ricky began his story on one of those rare occasions when he graced me with his company on our morning walk to school. In his mind there was something decidedly uncool about walking anywhere with your older sister and he would usually split off when we got closer to the school and take a separate entrance. Today was no exception.

"What are you going to do if you ever get a girlfriend?" I teased.

"That won't ever happen," he shot back. "Do you want to hear the story or not?"

He took my silence as an affirmative.

"On Saturday we were all hanging out at Andy's," he began, that funny look on his face a total giveaway that what was about to come was going to be, at least in his mind, a great tale. In the true spirit of an accomplished storyteller Ricky paused there for what seemed in interminable length of time.

"Yeah, yeah, and so…?" I retorted impatiently, finally giving in reluctantly to his absurd manipulation.

"Matt had some money, so he bought himself a bottle of Pepsi," Ricky continued. "Nick was there with us and he asked Matt if he could have a sip of his pop. Nick was broke, so he hadn't even bought any candy that he could trade, and Matt knew it."

At this point my brother paused again, but this time it was to chuckle to himself as he recalled what was to happen next. "Matt said, 'Sure'. Then making certain Nick was looking, spat in the top of the bottle and handed it to him with a big grin on his face."

"Yuck," I said with a puckish face. "What did Nick do?"

"Matt was surprised when Nick took the bottle, brought it up close to his mouth, spit in it himself, then passed it back."

My brother was delighting in the telling of the story, and obviously impressed with Nick. So was I, if I do say so. Like him as I did, Matt had it coming for that stunt.

"He just looked at his Pepsi," Ricky continued, "then at Nick, called him an effin asshole, put the bottle in the empty bottle rack and walked out. Matt was really pissed off, but he deserved it. It even got a smile out of old Andy."

By this time the story had me in such fits of laughter I practically dropped the homework binders and texts I was carrying. The anecdote was truly funny in its own right, but doubly so since the victim was Matt, who always seemed to be pulling off pranks and getting away with it.

It was Matt who came to school one morning wearing two completely different colored socks, and when the teacher brought that fact to his attention he simply looked down and, without even the slightest pause replied that he had another pair at home just like it.

"Do you think he did that deliberately?" I asked Ricky.

"I don't know," he replied. "It's Matt. What can I say?"

On another occasion Matt had neglected to do an English homework assignment that had to be turned in for marking. He explained in great, flowery detail to his teacher, Mr. Moretti, how he had been walking across the footbridge on his way to school and had tripped on a loose board on the bridge. The homework assignment slipped out of his hands and fell through a hole in the wire mesh on the bridge's side rail, landing in the creek.

"I'm going to accept that," said Mr. Moretti to everyone's surprise. "But only because I don't believe anyone could actually make up a yarn that preposterous. And if it's made up it's the best one I've heard in a long time. Redo the assignment and have it into me tomorrow."

Who couldn't like a guy like Matt or a teacher like Mr. Moretti who brought a great, sardonic sense of humor to his job?

Chapter 24

Jaguars and Silver Dollars

The sawmill that our father worked for was actually owned by a very wealthy Calgary businessman named Al Bannon, whose family fortune came not solely from lumber, but a whole range of business ventures. He was a hands on entrepreneur and as such we could expect him to make visits to Blairmore two or three times a year. He was an imposing figure of a man, obviously older than our dad and well over six feet tall. He was also a heavy drinker. As a frequent guest in our house he could, with a little help from our dad, make short work of a twenty-sixer of rye whiskey. These were the days when drinking and driving was no big deal. At the end of an evening of visiting dad would send him on his way back to his motel room at the Turtle Mountain Hotel a few miles down the road.

Mom used to swear that Mr. Bannon, which she

insisted was how we were to address him, came to the Pass simply to escape a rather miserable marriage to a reclusive and equally alcoholic wife. Mr. Bannon didn't mean much to me and I would usually sequester myself in my bedroom when he came to visit.

But Ricky loved him, and the feelings were reciprocated. I must add here, though, that my brother's fondness for Mr. Bannon, at least initially, was predicated more on material gain than on any other honest emotional bond. On each of his visits he would bring along an American silver dollar, which he made sure got into my brother's possession before he left.

Before each of his visits to our home our dad would say to us; more directed at my brother, "Now, listen. Mr. Bannon is here on business. You stay out of the living room when he gets here. We're talking and don't want to be interrupted with you kids running in and out and butting in."

I didn't really care and for his part my brother followed our dad's orders, if not entirely in the spirit in which they were intended. "Why don't you just come upstairs with me when he gets here?" I questioned my brother on one earlier occasion.

"Because we're friends, and I think he wants to see me," he responded, realizing, I think, that his partial truth didn't really cover up his covetous ways.

When everyone had said their hellos and were settled in the living room with drinks in hand Ricky would make sure that our visitor spotted him hanging out in the kitchen through the glass French door that separated the two rooms. My brother would make every pretense to be in the kitchen, and when Mr. Bannon spotted him he would halt whatever he was discussing with dad and signal my brother to come in to say hi, and chat a bit. This was always followed by him reaching into his pants pocket and pulling out the silver dollar, which he handed over to my brother with a simple, "Here, take this".

A little older and perhaps a little wiser I found it amusing that he always had one of those big American silver dollars tucked away in his pocket when he visited, as if a millionaire such as he just walked around every day with almost obsolete U.S. currency in his pocket. And those silver dollars were huge. You could almost serve dinner on them. I was amused and a little peeved, too, if the truth be known. He always just brought one and only for my brother. I guess I gave up the right to complain too much since I always disappeared when he came around, and he scarcely knew I existed.

"You think I just like Mr. Bannon for the silver dollars he gives me, don't you?" Ricky said to me one rainy afternoon as we mulled only half interestedly over a game of Monopoly; a game I might add, to which he always felt obliged to make up his own rules.

"Well, that's what it looks like to me," I responded. "Are you honestly going to tell me otherwise?"

"It's not like we're best buddies or anything," Ricky went on, "but I really do like him just for him."

"Exactly what does that mean?" I pressed. "He's dad's boss, you know, not our uncle, even though you like to refer to him as 'Uncle Al'. I thought dad told you to stop calling him that."

"I know, but I also know he likes me calling him Uncle Al. It's kind of like something we just share. I remember the first time I called him that. It was almost like an accident," my brother went on. "Remember a few years back when I had to go up to Calgary for my eye examination? I had to stay over a few days at the hospital that time, and dad had to get back to work. Mr. Bannon was coming down to the Pass that week anyway, so he told dad he'd pick me up at the hospital and bring me home."

"Yeah, I remember that," I admitted.

"Well, when he picked me up at the hospital the nurse that brought me out in the wheelchair said jokingly to me, 'Do you know this guy?'

"I looked way up at him and without even thinking said, 'Yup, he's my Uncle Al.' I never saw him smile like that before," Ricky added. "We walked out to the parking lot and his hand never left my shoulder, and somehow everything was different with us.

"Before we left Calgary we had to drop by his house so he could pick up his suitcase and he asked me if I wanted to come in or wait in the car. It was a big old house, almost like a mansion, so you know me, I wanted to see what it was like inside. It was pretty creepy, actually. The windows had these dark reddish velvet drapes. They were all closed and the place was really dark even though it was sunny outside. Mr. Bannon brought his wife,

Muriel, into the living room to meet me. She was really skinny and just had on this ugly, dark green housecoat. Her hair was messed up and it looked like she had just gotten out of bed. All she said to me was 'hi', and it sounded a little slurred. Even the way she was walking I was pretty sure she was drunk, and it wasn't even lunchtime.

"I sat there on this terribly uncomfortable old antique couch for about fifteen or twenty minutes," Ricky went on. "I could hear them in one of the other rooms and it sounded like they were having a pretty good row. Then Mr. Bannon came out with his suitcase and another small bag and we left. He looked really sad and I felt sorry for him. Nothing seemed right. We didn't say anything to each other until we were well out of Calgary. Finally, he said to me, 'How did the eye examination go, Ricky?'

"'Pretty good,' I replied, 'but Dr. Gorrell could tell right away that I hadn't been wearing my glasses regularly and gave me heck for that. I don't know how he can tell something like that, do you?'

"My new Uncle Al just shrugged his shoulders and replied, 'They have their ways.'

"'Dr. Gorrell says I have to get a new prescription because I've lost some vision in my bad eye,' I went on, not wanting to return to silence. 'I don't wear my glasses that much because I hate those wire-rimmed ones that mom makes me wear. I get teased a lot at school.'

"'Well, you have to take better care of your glasses then, Ricky,' he scolded kindly, somehow knowing my habit of yanking them off my face carelessly. 'Maybe I can talk to your mom about it, but remember, those plastic frames aren't made of rubber. You have to be more careful with them.'"

The duo was driving back to Blairmore in Mr. Bannon's brand new Jaguar Mark 1. Ricky thought the sleek chocolate brown sedan was beautiful, and in the 1950s Jaguar topped the list of sought-after exotic import cars. Like Triumph, MG, and Austin-Healy, they mostly hailed from England. One of Mr. Bannon's family business interests was ownership of British Auto Imports in Calgary, the city's Jaguar and MG dealership. So Mr. Bannon always drove a Jag, as they were popularly known.

My brother wasn't done relating the story of his trip with Uncle Al yet. I should have known that there'd be more. Nothing in my brother's life was ever quite that simple.

"We were getting pretty close to the Pass," Ricky went on. "We'd been chatting on and off for most of the way and Uncle Al had stopped at the truck stop near Fort Macleod and bought me a Coke and deluxe hamburger. I felt like a bit of a big shot driving into the truck stop in the Jag. When we came out of the diner there were three or four guys standing around admiring the car.

"Anyway, we got back on the road and about half an hour later we were coming up on that nasty S-corner at Burmis and I said to Uncle Al, 'I hear that no one can take that corner at a hundred miles an hour.'

"'Oh?' he said, 'And who told you that?'

"'I just heard it somewhere,' I replied. 'I heard that some guys had been killed on this corner.'

"'I don't doubt that,' Uncle Al replied, 'But they probably weren't driving a Jaguar.'

"'Jumping way ahead of myself, I said, "Can we do it?"

"'You won't tell your dad?' he replied.

"Nope," I said, feeling a real knot of excitement as we approached the corners.

"About a mile east Uncle Al began to accelerate the Jag. I watched the speedometer go from sixty, then to eighty and finally to ninety as we went into the curves. My eyes were darting between the road and the speedometer. Halfway through the first corner the speedometer hit the magic hundred mark. It dropped briefly back down to ninety, then hit a hundred again on the second curve. When we got through that second corner Uncle Al slowed it back down to sixty. He looked over at me with a grin on his face and said, 'Now remember, Ricky, your dad doesn't find out about this, right?'

"So, the only reason I'm telling you this is because you've never squealed on me and I trust you," Ricky cautioned. "Besides, that was a few years ago, anyway."

"This whole secrecy thing seems pretty one-sided to me," I retorted. "I have to keep all your secrets and you don't have to keep any of mine."

"Well Katty, why don't you get a few and try me out" he quipped back.

Sadly now, in hindsight, I never did.

The story of him and Uncle Al rang true to me. My brother's prevarication was generally reserved for getting him out of tough jams, and even then it was more like bending the truth to suit his needs. He didn't make up stories. He didn't have to. And it somewhat softened my belief that his relationship with his Uncle Al was wholly mercenary. I do say "his" Uncle Al, because I personally could never feel the closeness to him that my brother obviously did.

Chapter 25

Name Callin' and Smart Assn'

Ricky's soft spot for his Uncle Al pretty much characterized his personality. It takes a special sort of person, I think, to hold such empathy at so young an age. How could someone so young understand that loneliness and unhappiness could result in alcoholism? I'm not sure whether this was inborn or, at least in part, a learned response. My brother certainly had a dose of the latter.

"Kids can be cruel" is more than a hack, overused phrase, I think. I saw more than my share of it in a neighborhood teeming with children aged from preschoolers to teens, and to be certain I found myself, as the quiet and reserved one, on the receiving end of some very callous and hurtful barbs.

In his early elementary school years my brother, almost overnight, became one of those snot-nosed little buggers whose newly discovered cockiness spewed out endlessly and marked him as a real little mouthpiece. I don't know what brought it on, but I suspect it had something to do with some of the teasing he had taken earlier. The whole bad attitude thing was short lived, thank heavens, but I wish it had ended on a little better note than it did.

"Your big yap is going to get you into some real trouble someday," I warned him. "Lots of the older kids think you're nothing but a little jerk." Were he not my brother, I would have probably detested him myself. At best he could be hard to take and he certainly tested my affections. His response to my warning was completely in step with his obnoxious arrogance.

"Shut up, Katty," he chirped back at me, "I'll say whatever I want."

Then one day it happened.

It was a Saturday afternoon in early summer and, typical of a warm summer Saturday, the neighborhood was filled with groups of kids playing. Mom and dad were out doing their weekly grocery shopping and my friend Marlene and I were playing hopscotch on the sidewalk in front of our house.

"Is that Ricky?" Marlene said to me as she cast a glance up the block.

It was hard to tell at first because he was hobbling down the street, bent over holding his stomach with one hand and his other one covering one eye. But it was my brother all right, determined only by the fact that it was the same striped t-shirt he was wearing when he left the house that morning.

As he drew closer I could tell that it was pretty serious. Blood was running from his nose and it was all over the front of him. I could see a big purplish welt on one cheek. His upper lip was split open and he still held his hand over his other eye.

"What happened to you?" I screeched, my obvious panic registering in the shrill tone of my voice.

Ricky said nothing, staring vacantly towards our house. I repeated the question at least three more times and got nothing.

"Where were you?" I questioned at last.

"Over in the alley behind Wayne Coburne's place," my brother said after a long pause. I knew that was pretty much all that I was going to get out of him.

Alleys were the playgrounds of the 1950s. It's where the local kids could play hide and seek, kick the can, cops and robbers, cowboys and Indians, or any number of other games of their own invention. Why not? The alleys provided access to a ready-made maze of old shacks, abandoned outhouses, broken-down wooden fences, ash and trash boxes, old single-car garages and dozens of narrow openings between all of these. In addition, most of the people whose houses backed onto these alleys didn't much mind the kids coming and hiding in their yards, so long as they didn't steal or break anything or trample in their gardens. Any given alley in town provided a hundred hiding places. And there wasn't a single metal trash can lid that wasn't beaten to a pulp having been used as a "shield" in some playful juvenile sword fight.

It was pretty obvious to me, though, that Ricky hadn't been playing at any of those games.

"Marlene, can you take my brother in the house and clean him up a bit?" I asked. "I'll be right back. I'm going over to Wayne's place to find out exactly what happened here."

Wayne Coburne was my age. He never knew it, but I was always a little bit sweet on him. He lived two blocks away from us and was part of that older "in" group of boys that Ricky and his buddies were always aspiring to be part of, never quite making the cut. It's amazing the difference a year or so makes when you're a kid.

I caught up to Wayne, still in the alley behind his place with three or four of his friends, tossing a football around. I think he could tell by my approach that I was livid and he would have some answering to do.

"What happened to my brother, Wayne?" I demanded, not even bothering with the courtesy of a greeting.

"It wasn't all our fault," he replied with a tone of defensiveness, though not completely avoiding a degree of responsibility. "It was Koko and Arnaud."

Koko and Arnaud Grenier were twin brothers; big heavy boys, a year older than my brother, and each of them were half again his size. They were both mentally handicapped, Koko considerably moreso than Arnaud. The Grenier family had moved to Blairmore about the same time as we had, but no one saw the two boys very often because they didn't go to school. They lived in an old, rundown house across the alley from the Coburne's with their divorced mother.

"You know what your brother's like," Wayne went on. "always the little Smart Alec. He was teasing both of the boys, calling them 'retards' and really making fun of them in front of everyone. My brother Robbie and I decided we'd pretty much had enough of it, so we grabbed him and tied him up to that telephone pole over there. Then we told Koko and Arnaud that they could go ahead and beat him up.

"At first they were both just pushing at him a bit. We thought it was pretty funny; the look on your brother's face. Then Koko really started punching hard. He hit Ricky a few times in the stomach then started really punching him like crazy all over his face and head. Kicking him, too. Then Arnaud started in. Ricky was yelling and crying at the same time and things got really crazy. We tried to stop the twins, but it was like they didn't even hear us. We tried to pull Koko away, but that just seemed to make him madder. We thought they were going to kill him. Ricky was trying to break loose, but we had him tied up pretty good.

"Mrs. Grenier must have heard all the commotion and came running out into the alley screaming at her boys to stop. They did, but not before Koko gave your brother one last good kick. Mrs. Grenier took the boys back in the house and was swearing over her shoulder at us all the way, telling us that she was going to call the cops and everything. We untied Ricky. He was still crying and we could tell he was really hurt. He never said one word to us, just turned around and left."

I stood there speechless. I couldn't believe what had happened, though I knew my brother had been cruising for trouble for quite some time. The thought of him possibly being beaten to death for it had never even crossed my mind. How could it have?

When I got back home Marlene had him pretty much cleaned up, but he still looked a mess. He was standing in the kitchen without his bloodied t-shirt on and I could see the welts already showing on his stomach and chest. His face already looked like those old black and white pictures you see of professional boxers after a fight. His right eye was swollen shut and already turning purple. But miraculously his nose, though still bleeding slightly, didn't seem to be broken and he wasn't missing any teeth.

That day my brother became a different person; a brother far easier to love. The way that it happened really had upset me, but I can honestly say that I was glad for the change it had brought about.

I went upstairs and got him a fresh t-shirt from his dresser, brought it back down, and Marlene and I helped pull it on over his swollen, painful looking face. Then I smiled at him in my most gentle and sisterly way and said, "Well, this is one we won't be keeping from the folks."

He looked back at me through his one eye that wasn't swollen shut and said, "Did you find my glasses?"

"Yes," I replied. "Wayne's brother had them, but they're all bust up... yet again. Mom isn't going to be very happy with you."

"What are we going to tell mom and dad?" he asked, worried less now about his wounds than the consequences facing him.

"We're going to tell them the truth, Ricky," I said. "They're not stupid. It's obvious you've been beaten up and they'll know it as soon as they look at you. You were teasing those poor Grenier boys and though you didn't deserve what they did to you, you certainly deserved something."

My brother held his head in shame, and I knew this time that it was real and I felt a pang of sisterly compassion.

"Go up to your room and stay up there when the folks get home," I ordered. "I will explain everything to them, including your name calling. If they come home and see you looking like this when they walk through the door they're going to go ballistic. I'll try to break it to them more gently, but they're going to get the truth."

I did. Mom cried when she went upstairs and looked at Ricky's bloated, discolored face and the bruises all over his chest and shoulders. Being an amateur boxer in his youth dad took it more as a life lesson, particularly after hearing the details from me: no broken bones, no missing teeth.

As well, this time Ricky would be paying for the repairs to his glasses out of his paper route money. I smiled inwardly when I heard that pronouncement.

Chapter 26

The "James" Saga

I may have made mention, in passing, of my brother's innate entrepreneurial instincts oft bordering on outright opportunism. For a brief period, Ricky and a few of his friends were invited to join a local go-cart club. The club itself was the brainchild of Mr. Jacobs (I never did know his first name), a newcomer to the Pass, who had an interest in the sport and thought it a great way to teach some of the local kids a bit about mechanics and getting them to possibly develop some driving skills along the way.

Mr. Jacobs had already built two carts, each powered by some old Briggs & Stratton gas engines he'd found somewhere. I'm probably making too much of this club business, because in the end it was a whimpering failure. Mr. Jacobs, not having any sons of his own, did not quite grasp the subtle workings of the adolescent male brain. He had only one child himself and that was his daughter, Hazel, who I hung around with a bit. He can be forgiven for failing to understand that strict rules seldom coalesce well with young, overactive adolescents; that being especially so when you put them in a group together and give them a weapon like a go-cart.

And, on that note, I shall move on, for often a story left untold becomes all the more enticing as one's own imagination is allowed to fill in the gaps. Besides, it is only germane in that it sets the stage for my account of The James. Yes, THE James, for I am not referring to a person here.

Mr. Jacobs kept his go-carts in his big double car garage when they weren't being used and the boys in the club would often gather there to learn the ins and outs of the four-stroke engine. He was a rather portly, congenial fellow who appeared to love his big, spacious, well-equipped garage as much as he did his house. He must have, because that's where you'd usually find him tinkering with one thing or another. He was a born teacher even though he wasn't one, and Ricky and his friends all learned a lot from their brief time with him and the club.

On one such occasion Ricky noticed, back in a

dark corner of the garage, an old, vintage motorcycle under an old blanket and leaning against a wall because it had no kickstand of its own. The tires were both flat and it was covered in dust, looking sadly like it hadn't seen the light of day in years. Across the side of the dull burgundy gas tank in faded gold lettering was the insignia "James" between two outstretched eagle wings. My brother's curiosity got the best of him as it often did, and he asked Mr. Jacobs about the machine.

"Oh, it's an old World War II English motorcycle that I picked up eight or ten years ago from a guy I knew," he replied. "I thought it was pretty neat when I bought it, but I've never paid much attention to it since, other than to know that it isn't working. I've never had it running myself, but the guy who sold it to me swore there was nothing really wrong with it mechanically."

For Ricky's part, he cared little whether it worked or not. He had just fallen in love for the first time--with the way it looked, with those big fat tires, with the teardrop gas tank and that single, low-slung seat, almost like those Harleys in that old movie with Marlon Brando, perhaps just a tad smaller.

Feigning only mild interest in the story, which

barely concealed his excitement, Ricky squeaked out, "Would you be willing to sell it?"

Mr. Jacobs looked at him with a small smile and said, "I don't know. I told you it's not working and I'm not certain that it ever will. It hasn't run for years. I'd hate to sell you something that's broken." He stood there for a moment in thought, not missing the disappointment registered on Ricky's face. "Y'know," he said finally, "it might just be a great learning experience for you, trying to get the old girl going again. Yeah, it's yours if you've got fifteen bucks to spare. That's what I paid for it."

Ricky wasted no time, fearful that Mr. Jacobs might just change his mind for any number of reasons. He jumped on his bike and was home in five minutes flat. He rushed upstairs to where his paper route money was kept in a tin box and grabbed up a ten- and five-dollar bill, stuffing them hastily into his pocket on his way down the stairs. He knew he couldn't take his bike back to the Jacobs' house because he'd have to push his newly-acquired treasure all the way back home with two flattened tires.

When he got back one of the big double doors was still open and Mr. Jacobs was standing there waiting for him. "Good news, Ricky," he said. "I started my compressor and pumped up the tires. It looks like both of them are in pretty good shape and holding air. It's going to make it a lot easier to push home."

My brother hastily handed over the ten and five, a month's profit from his paper route, but probably little more than a token of good faith on Mr. Jacobs' part.

"Remember, Ricky," he said as a parting note, "if you ever do get this thing working, it's a two-stroke engine not a four-stroke like those engines on the go carts. You'll have to mix the gas and oil before you put it in the gas tank, just like your dad's lawn mower. And, whatever you do, don't remove the muffler. Those two-stroke engines need the back-pressure to work properly. If you run it with the muffler off you'll burn out the engine."

Whether he had his dad's permission or not, Ricky was now the proud owner of his very own motorcycle. It was, in a word cool, with its low profile look, not like those flat-top Hondas and Suzukis that were all the current rage. Working or not, my brother spent a few hours just cleaning and scraping the black, crusted-on oil off his new toy, caring little, it seemed, whether the beast would ever run at all.

There really was no old fuel to drain off. The tank was completely empty and probably had been for quite some time. Ricky spent the better part of three days with his friend Nick taking the motor completely apart and putting it back together again, cleaning every piece meticulously. They had fudged some of his dad's lawnmower fuel in order to test their handiwork. The real culprit, he and Nick determined, was probably the spark plug. It had become so coated with black soot that there was virtually no spark gap at all. They cleaned that off with an SOS pad from under mom's kitchen sink, then set the gap in the plug the width of dad's hacksaw blade.

With a couple of deep, pensive breaths Ricky kicked viciously on the kick-starter. Nothing. Again. Nothing. Then, a third, fourth and fifth time in rapid succession and still nothing. On the sixth kick there was a brief sputter from the engine. On the seventh the motor, probably idle for longer than Ricky and Nick had been alive, fired up, belching a cloud of stinking blue smoke from its peashooter-sized exhaust pipe. The two of them sat there gleefully revving the engine, oblivious to the pall of blue exhaust that enveloped them and drifted over the entire back yard. That afternoon marked the real beginning of what I came to call "The James Saga". As quiet and unassuming as I was I always had a keen sense of what could get my brother's goat.

If the boys' mechanical success concerned my father he never really let on. He was a lover of motorcycles himself and had owned a number of them in his youth, including a Harley and an Indian. A disciplinarian in his own right, he was also somewhat dismissive of laws that he found personally and unnecessarily burdensome. The fact that The James was not equipped with headlight, tail lights, signal lights or horn, all of which were legal requirements for road usage, did not register with him as any serious impediment to riding the motorcycle around the neighborhood. To his credit, he did caution Ricky and his friends on the risk of taking it out on the highway.

Because Nick had worked with my brother at getting the machine working, Ricky agreed to sell him a half share in The James for ten dollars. Do you see now what I mean about entrepreneurial?

As is the case in a small town, interest grew rapidly in The James and when they took it out for a run around the neighborhood, or up into the bush on one of the back trails, four or five of their buddies would tag along and want to take it for a spin as well. Seeing no real gain in that, Ricky and Nick decided to sell user shares in their motorcycle for five dollars per person, netting them another twenty dollars. Users could only ride The James when the two core partners decided to take it out, which was actually quite frequently, so everyone got value for their money.

Things were going pretty well; probably too well. Then the crap hit the fan. One early evening Matt, who had bought a user share, was taking the bike for a spin up the main drag in our neighborhood when a Mountie cruiser appeared at an intersection two blocks ahead. Ricky, Nick and a few others who were waiting their turn to ride stood a few blocks behind and watched as things unfolded before them. Spotting the cop car Matt diverted into an alley, but it was already too late. He'd been spotted. With flashers on the Mountie followed him into the alley. Matt braked the motorcycle, threw it down as it was still running, and strolled nonchalantly into the nearest yard presenting the appearance that he knew nothing of what was going on right behind him. It was quite possibly the worst subterfuge ever attempted by anyone, ever.

The cop yelled loudly to Matt and ordered him back into the alley. Pointing to The James he enquired, "Is this yours?" to which Matt, in absolute honesty, answered in the negative. "Do you have a driver's license?" drew yet another negative.

"I have to tell you," said the Mountie, "that everything I see here right now is illegal. You have no license, and the motorcycle lacks virtually every safety feature required of it. I count at least six offences here all of which carry fairly stiff fines."

Noting Matt's youth and the fact that he could likely ill afford even one of the penalties, the Mountie continued. "I'm going to give you a break tonight, son," he continued. "I don't know who owns this piece of crap, but I want you to let him know that if I see it being operated again on the streets of Blairmore there will be fines handed out for each and every offence. I will be letting my fellow officers know of this warning as well."

The bike was still lying there on its side and running noisily. "Now shut that thing off and walk it back to where ever it came from," the Mountie ordered.

Matt was relieved, but visibly shaken by the encounter as the cop got back in his car and backed out of the dead end alley.

"The James Saga" was about to end-or was it?

Nope, not quite yet. There was still one more chapter yet to write. Ricky, Nick and the others knew it was the end for them. But what was to be done about the motorcycle itself? Those who merely had user shares cared little. They'd had their fun and were content to walk away from the whole affair and not be stupid enough to ask for any of their money back.

The fate of the little group of pals and their brush with the law spread quickly and brought with it a stroke of luck. Wee Jordie Murphy lived on a small acreage with his brother, sister and divorced mom on the north edge of town. Unlike my brother, who merely appeared to be on the wimpy side, Wee Jordie really was, on top of the fact that he was also just a little bit slimy. Over the summer Ricky had graciously given him one ride on the motorcycle and he, being a little younger, was thrilled by the experience.

"I'll buy the bike from you," he told Ricky one afternoon when they ran into one another downtown. "I can legally ride it on our property. How much you asking?"

With not a second thought Ricky told Jordie he'd let him have it for $25.00. Not taking him too seriously since he was so young, my brother and Nick gave the matter no more thought, but two days later he appeared and handed over the money. Ricky and Nick both suspected that he'd probably stolen it from his mother's purse, but decided wisely to ask no questions and they split the $25.00 between them. Twenty-five bucks was a pretty fair chunk of change back then. Jordie took the motorcycle and pushed it, with some effort due to his small stature, back home, uphill all the way. My brother's net take for the whole affair was just shy of forty dollars and Nick wasn't complaining because he did better than break even, thanks largely to Jordie's contribution.

Two weeks after the sale went down my brother and Nick ran into Jordie's older brother, Larry, and enquired as to the fate of their beloved James. "My brother thought it sounded crappy," said Larry, "so he removed the muffler to make it sound louder and tougher. He was running it up a slope back of our house last week and it just quit. It won't start and hasn't run since."

"Oh yeah," Ricky said under his breath to Nick, "We forgot to tell him about that."

Chapter 27

The Swimming Lesson

You can't rightly live up in the mountains and ignore the fact that, in additional to innumerable small alpine lakes, there is an almost endless web of rivulets, streams, and creeks, all feeding into rivers that flow out of the mountains and feed into other larger rivers. In the Pass every town had its favorite creek. In our case it was Lyons Creek which flowed down from the high pass south of town, through the southeast corner of Blairmore and into the Crowsnest River; the watery backbone of the Pass that started at Crowsnest Lake, less than two miles east of the summit of the Pass. But, hey, that's enough with the alpine geography lesson.

Lyons Creek was, indeed, a jewel. It was not necessarily that pretty, though, as it passed through town. By late summer that section of the creek turned into a dry, rock-strewn creek bed with no water in it whatsoever. But if you walked up the creek bed less than half a mile or so, everything changed. There you would find innumerable waterfalls and pools as you rounded nearly every bend.

None of the falls were ever given a real name. Each of the falls was designated simply by number, running from Third Falls up to Twenty-Seconds. No one could really determine where the first two falls actually were, or if they existed at all. That had always remained a bit of a mystery. Many could barely be placed into the classification of falls; the ultimate determiner being the presence of even the slightest hint of visible white water tumbling over an obstruction of some sort. The two favorites were Seventeens and Eighteens Falls, the latter edging out by a slight margin because it had the largest and deepest pool below the falls and a few choice rock promontories from which to jump or dive.

The window of opportunity to actually swim in the creek was perhaps six weeks; the last part of July and all of August. At any other time, the water was simply too intolerably cold as it was probably wet snow a short distance further up the creek. Even drinking it would bring on immediate brain freeze, as we used to like to call it. But even in July and August—the swimming season—jumping right into the water cold turkey was scarcely an option. The body had to adjust, ever so slowly, to the cold. Standing in the shallows up to the knees often resulted in total paralysis of your feet, which remarkably went away once your whole body was immersed. That was probably due to an accelerated heartbeat pumping blood down to the extremities in a desperate attempt by the body to keep itself alive.

Swim in it they did; all of them driven on by peer pressure and the accompanying fact that there was always at least one of them foolish enough to be the first one in. Ricky used to laugh at my red-faced embarrassment when he'd comment that swimming at "Eighteens" always turned guys into girls, referring, as I knew, to the shrinking effects the combination of ice cold water and tight swimming suits had on certain parts of the male anatomy.

It was at Eighteens that Ricky practically met his demise, yet again. This time the story didn't come from him, probably because he knew that doing so would bring me to tears. My brother, kind as he was to me, had real difficulty dealing with my rare but genuine emotional outbursts. He knew that the swimming incident would certainly have had that effect on me. So he kept quiet, secure in the belief that I'd never find out. But I did, and Ricky's friend, Stevie, was the culprit this time. He had let the story slip out by innocently asking me how Ricky was doing. It didn't take much for me to divine the reason for such a question. Poor Stevie was left to face the embarrassment of my tears, no doubt wishing that he, too, had kept his mouth shut.

Now my little brother was in big trouble with me on two accounts; one, for his stupidity and two, for his futile attempt at keeping it from me.

Five or six of them had decided to take the walk up to Eighteens Falls and go for a swim. It was around the first of August and the water was going to be about as warm as it was ever going to get. It was scorching hot outside. Most of the guys knew how to swim in a fashion.

Allen Dixon was new to Blairmore, having arrived with his family late the previous summer. Being quite outgoing, it wasn't long before he fell in with my brother and his cohorts and became one of the guys. Allen, who hailed from somewhere out on the prairies, admitted that he'd never learned to swim, but he wanted to tag along with his new-found friends, anyway.

"We told Allen that swimming was simple and that when we got to the falls we'd give him a lesson and have him doing it in no time at all," Stevie confessed to me.

"Okay, okay," I said impatiently. "What exactly happened?"

"Well, we decided that the best thing to do was to have Ricky and Nick wade into the water on either side of Allen. Then when they were deep enough the plan was to give him a big shove toward the rock ledge on the other side of the pool so he could dog paddle to it. You've been there yourself, Kathryn," Stevie went on. "There's only twelve or fifteen feet of deep water before you get to the ledge. We gave Allen a quick dry land lesson on how to dog paddle then the plan went into action."

"Yes," I interrupted caustically, "teaching someone how to swim out of water is always a really good idea." I think I was actually trying to stall hearing the details that were about to unfold.

"Anyway," Stevie continued, ignoring my sarcasm, "when they got chest-deep in the water Allen was getting a little bit scared and the sandy slope on the bottom of the pool got a lot steeper. Ricky and Nick lost their footing and were quickly in over their heads. Allen had been holding onto them for dear life, and when their heads went under the water he panicked and just grabbed onto their hair and held on for dear life. He started screaming like crazy and we could see that he was holding Nick and Ricky down under the water just to keep himself afloat."

Stevie continued, "I don't know if Ricky and Nick have some sort of secret communication, but they actually got themselves turned around both at the same time, in spite of Allen's death grip on their hair, and swam underwater back to the shallower part of the pool where they could get their footing back and walk the rest of the way out. When they were back on shore the first thing Nick did was punch Allen right in the face, even though the whole thing was probably not his fault at all."

"There's no 'probably' about it," I snarled back at Stevie, the tears now streaming down my face.

All through dinner that night I glared across the table at Ricky but said nothing. He knew he was in for an earful from me, and right after dishes he darted out the back door to avoid me. But he couldn't stay out forever and when he got back home he found me sitting on the edge of his bed... waiting.

That was the night that my angry yelling brought mom running upstairs in a panic, thinking that something awful had happened to me. In the throes of my anguish and anger at my brother's irresponsibility I covered for him yet again, telling mom that we'd just had a big argument over some other petty matter. I'm sure she knew better, gauging the degree of my distress, but she was also acutely aware of the protective shell that Ricky and I were able to put around ourselves to shield us from the outside. The "outside." How strange that I chose to use that term?

In hindsight, I think that mom, a very wise woman in her own right, used me as some sort of surrogate in the discipline of her youngest. She knew, I'm sure, that disappointing me was harder on Ricky than any form of punishment that she could have meted out.

The tight relationship shared between my brother and me was a precarious one however, and no one knew that better than I. His unwillingness to tell me about the swimming incident was, to me, a crack in our solidarity. It was a crack that bothered me deeply, mostly because of its duality. On one hand I would be quite content not to be privy to many of the things that happened to him, and I was aware that he knew that. On the other hand, on those rare times when he did keep something from me and I found out in some other way I felt totally betrayed. Yet I knew it wasn't real betrayal, but Ricky's way of either protecting me or shielding himself from my wrath. The problem had always been that I was never quite certain which one it was, and that bothered me the most.

Looking back now, it was likely my desire to control things colliding head on with Ricky's penchant for living in what I believed to be a completely turbulent world of his own making. That controlling part of my personality would be content in having the option to say "tell me" or "don't tell me." That choice had never been mine to make, and somewhere along the way I began to understand that my brother—my little brother—was in complete control of our relationship and always had been.

Chapter 28

A "Plunge" Into Darkness

Mom and dad let Ricky go on a Saturday night sleepover at Donny MacArthur's place. Now you might be thinking, "What's wrong with that? Kids have sleepovers all the time."

Everything! That's what's wrong with that.

Nothing good ever came from putting Ricky Callaghan together with Donny MacArthur. Throwing Donny's younger brother, Stewy, into the mix virtually guaranteed chaos. The MacArthur house was a huge, two-story affair; originally built as a residence for single female teachers in the years when such was the custom. So there you have it; all the right ingredients for trouble—three young boys, lack of sleep, minimal supervision and nothing better to do.

And sure enough...

I wasn't expecting my brother home until sometime Sunday afternoon, noon at the earliest, so I was enjoying the quiet time his absence was providing me. It was just before nine when I heard a bit of a buzz of conversation coming from the downstairs kitchen; then the footsteps coming up the stairs, their very cadence telling me that something had gone quite poorly. After years, you become sensitized to these things, so I knew immediately not to expect him to come rushing into my room to fill me in on the fun night he'd had over at his friend's house. No, he was going straight to his room and making me come to him. It was more than I could bear to try and wait him out, so half an hour later found me tapping meekly at the entryway to his room.

"Yeah, come on in," I heard him say, almost dismissively. As I entered he was sitting up against the headboard of his bed and looking intently at the watch on his wrist. I knew exactly what that meant. He'd won the waiting game and he wanted to make sure I knew it.

"Home a bit early, aren't you?" I ventured. "What? Did the MacArthurs all have to go to church this morning?" I inquired facetiously, with a small, knowing grin I could barely suppress.

"Shut up," said Ricky. "I think I could be in real hot water this time, and it might even end up costing me some money."

My curiosity bloomed like a Morning Glory. But I dampened my eagerness to learn more and let my brother tell it at his own pace and in his own way, which I knew would include volumes of superfluous introductory detail.

"Donny's house is huge, but it's really a dump," he started. "Some of those old places haven't been fixed up in years. The downstairs is pretty nice, but the upstairs really isn't. Donny's folks don't even sleep up there. Their bedroom is on the main floor off the living room. I hadn't ever been up there before last night. Worn linoleum, walls and ceilings full of cracks like spider webs, just like that crap dad stripped off the walls when he was fixing this place up a few years ago. Remember that? He hauled truckloads of that shit out of here then replaced it with that nice wood grain paneling we have now."

Frankly, this was a bit more preamble than I was prepared for and my endurance was wearing thin. The fact that Ricky felt the necessity for such a lengthy and circuitous introduction made me realize this one was going to be a gooder, so I contained my annoyance.

Finally, the subject, for no apparent reason, changed from home renovation to bathroom amenities. "Did you know that they have a complete upstairs bathroom in Donny's house?"

I gave him a rather neutral nod, not knowing exactly where this whole thing was going.

"Yeah, they've had some trouble with the toilet so they have to keep one of those toilet plungers beside it all the time, just in case it plugs up and overflows. It's kind of like the one dad has in the basement, only theirs has orange rubber."

Ah ha, we were getting warmer. I could feel it. "Well, lots of people keep their plungers in their bathrooms," I volunteered, knowing full well now that the plunger was the real key to the rest of this tale. "So what's that got to do with anything?"

Donny, Stewey and I got up pretty early this morning and we were just horsing around in the upstairs hallway," he said, "y'know, wrestling and stuff like that, nothing serious. Donny grabbed his mom's broom and was pretending it was a lance and poking me with it. I was backing up and looked into the bathroom. That's when I spotted the plunger, so I ran in and grabbed it to even the odds.

"Really, we were just faking everything. Donny stood with his back against the hallway wall and I pretended to lunge at him with the plunger. I deliberately missed him, of course, but the plunger stuck to the wall right next to him, just like that suction cup dart gun I had a few years ago. You remember that gun, don't you?"

"Yeah, yeah," I acknowledged rather impatiently, "so you stuck a dirty toilet plunger on the wall. No big deal. It probably lost its suction and fell off by itself before you even got home."

"Hold it, I'm not done yet," Ricky interrupted. "When I went to pull the plunger off the wall, a huge, and I mean a really huge, chunk of that crappy plaster came with it, at least three feet by three feet. It broke all over the floor and you could see the exposed lath underneath where the plaster had been. I almost shit myself. None of us knew what to do, so Donny told me it was probably best if I just grabbed my stuff and got out before his folks woke up. I'm pretty sure that he and Stewy will take the blame for it, but when I was walking home thinking about it, it dawned on me that by leaving I was pretty much admitting my guilt. I think I'm just going to stay in my room today and read some comics. I'll find out from Donny what happened when I get to school tomorrow."

Walking back to school together after lunch on Monday, Ricky was uncharacteristically quiet, and frankly I'd waited long enough. I said, "Well, what did Donny say?"

"He told me that he had to tell his folks the truth," my brother replied, with a note of resignation. "Donny started out by saying that the plaster must have fallen off the wall by itself during the night. His parents didn't buy that one. Of course, the fact that I'd left and gone home even before breakfast was a real red flag for his mom, so it didn't take her long to drag the truth out of them. Stewy, the little rat, caved in like a snow fort in April."

I couldn't help smiling at this simile, especially since I knew what an arrogant and annoying little jerk Stewy could be.

"So now what?" I asked.

"Donny didn't say. His dad is going to find a professional plasterer to repair the damage. He told me his family is moving back to Scotland next year and will be selling the house, so his dad doesn't want to undertake any major renovation to the place. There'll be no more sleepovers, for sure, and I've already let Donny and his brother know that I won't likely be coming around for a visit any time soon."

"Oh, you chicken," I jested, which drew only the slightest smile from my brother and pretty much punctuated the conversation.

Chapter 29

The Summer of the Philistines

Girls will find an article like a rubber band, for example, and do something useful with it: tie up their hair, wrap it around their loose pile of Valentines cards from school. You get the drift. Boys will find that same rubber band and turn it into a weapon. That's just what boys do every time, guaranteed.

It should not have come as any surprise, then, that we were about to experience "The Summer of the Philistines". Being as most of the families in our corner of town were Italian, and thus almost by definition Catholics, it was only a matter of time before my brother's friends picked up on the Biblical story of David and Goliath. It was a nice story, especially the part about David's choice of weaponry.

Almost without exception our fathers worked

in the mines, sawmills, or some other related industrial job. Every household had one or two pairs of old, used up work boots kicking about; work boots with nice big leather tongues in them. On a good day those boots might even have the laces still in them, but never to mind because if they didn't there were always skate laces. After all, it was summer, and who needs to use their skates in the summer? Just a bit of boy reasoning here.

Within a few days five or six of the guys had fashioned themselves stone slings, just like David had when he took on Goliath in the Bible story. Well, not quite. Some were better than others and it took another few days to perfect them. Blairmore had to face the grim prospect of a gang of seriously irresponsible hooligans armed with seriously dangerous weapons.

"You better not be playing in town with that thing," I warned my brother when he showed his off to me. "You could really hurt someone or break a window or something. Remember what happened with that slingshot you made a few years ago."

"Don't worry," he assured me. "We're going to practice up at the lime pits. We can fire the stones

223

up against that big cliff there and not hurt any-thing."

From experience, I greeted my brother's reas-surances with a practical degree of skepticism, but really there was little I could do to stop him or his friends anyway. After all, they hadn't really hurt anyone... yet. To me, 'don't worry' meant exactly the opposite.

The boys were having a great time with their newfound sport. One afternoon Ricky invited me up to the lime pits to see how good they had all become. To be honest, I was quite amazed. They all handled their slings like pros, especially Chris Santoro, who from fifty yards could consistently hit a two-foot square target on the sheer stone wall. I breathed a sigh of relief. Maybe this wasn't going to be so bad after all.

I should have held that breath.

Slinging stones at high speed against a solid stone wall in the lime quarry and watching them shatter into a hundred pieces soon lost its luster, and Ricky and company were looking for new chal-lenges. The lime pit area was actually a height of land overlooking the railway, highway and Crowsnest River, all in that order.

"Y'know, Chris has the best throwing arm of all of us, and he made the best sling," my brother admitted to me rather reluctantly a few days after my foray to the pit with him and his pals. It was something I already knew, but I kept my silence. I do that when I sense that more is coming.

"Yesterday we were up in the pits and Chris said he was going to try and see if he could actually sling a rock as far as the river. We didn't think he could, and we all bet him two bits each that he couldn't. He picked up a nice round one, a little bigger than a golf ball, put it in the sling and let it go with a resounding snap. The rock actually landed right in the middle of the river, travelling so fast we could barely see the splash.

"I should have known better than to try and outdo him, but I bet him my quarter back that I could," my brother admitted. "Chris can throw a baseball almost twice as far as I can. He's just a natural. Plus, the laces on his sling are at least three inches longer than mine. I don't know what I was thinking.

"I picked a rock about the same size as his, put it in my sling and gave it all I had. The rock went way higher in the air than Chris's had, so I knew it wasn't going to get anywhere near the river. It was still in the air when we noticed a car down on the highway, heading west towards town. We just stood there watching. Even from as far away as we were we could hear the sound of the rock when it hit the hood of the car, then bounced straight into the windshield.

"All of us ran and ducked behind some rocks, pretty sure we'd smashed the windshield. The driver pulled over and got out, checked the damage to his car and looked up towards where we were hiding. He looked up our way for a long time, and we thought that he might have somehow spotted us. None of us moved a muscle. We waited there until he finally got back in his car and drove off.

"Then we went home... the long way. We all circled halfway around town through the bush and came down near the dump. We didn't want anyone to see us coming from the lime pit area, just in case that guy had reported it to the police."

"What did I tell you, you idiots?" I spat out. "What if that rock had gone through his windshield and you'd really hurt or killed that guy? Or, he could have had little kids in the car with him. Did you ever think of that? And, while I'm at it, did it ever dawn on you morons that other people might have seen you all going into the lime pits, swinging those slings around like you always do? If that guy reports it, you can be sure it won't be long before the police are knocking on our door."

In his typical fashion my tirade met with a blank, mute stare. Both questions went unanswered, with the only positive outcome being the conclusion of any further Biblical reenactments. If I had truly been holding my breath on this one, I could finally exhale.

Chapter 30

Getting His Money's Worth

Chris's uncle, Vittorio, was a crusty old charac-
ter whose lack of desire for conversation would
have you believing him to be unfriendly. Truth is,
he just didn't have a whole lot to say. He was so
much older than Chris's own dad that he could easily have passed as Chris's grandfather. With all of
the cousins, uncles and nephews I often had difficulty figuring out who was who in the Santoro
family.

"That old Vittorio seems like a real crab," I
commented to my brother one day as we were going past his place, walking down the railway tracks
on our way to Crazy Joe's Pond. Vittorio, who
lived within spitting distance of the pond and the
tracks as well, was sitting on a bench near the back
door of his rather ramshackle old house, puffing on
a cigar and taking in the warm afternoon as we

walked by.

Ricky ignored my comment, waved at the old bachelor and yelled, "Hi, Vito," as we went by. Barely acknowledging our presence one hand went up briefly, almost like he was shooing away a fly.

"He's alright," my brother finally responded. "You have to get to know him a bit. I thought he was that way, too, at first, but he just doesn't ever say very much. Chris and I have gone there to see him a few times when Chris's mom had baked some zeppola for him. He likes his pastries and that's about the only time you'll ever actually see him smile. But he's okay. He let Chris and us guys use the loft in his old log barn as a clubhouse until it got torn down last year."

"You guys actually have a club?" I questioned, mostly in jest. "And what, exactly, does your club do?" I had clearly caught him off guard.

"We, uh, used to go there and just talk and stuff. Nick brought over some magazines that we looked at."

"Oh, you mean like Popular Mechanics and Outdoor Life?" I suggested saucily, giving him a sly wink.

Ricky was clearly uncomfortable with my line

of questioning, so I let it drop, and he was quick to change the subject.

"Did I ever tell you about the cigars?"

"The cigars?" I replied. "No, I don't remember you saying anything about any cigars. Do I really want to hear about this?" I asked, knowing full well that he viewed that question only as an annoying interruption.

"Old Vittorio smokes those awful smelling Marco Gallo cigars," he started. "You've probably seen them. They're the ones that Dobek's Store has in that glass container behind the counter; the ones that are all bent and twisted and look like a stack of dried up old sticks. His whole house reeks of them."

"Those are cigars?" I replied with a distasteful curled up lip. "I thought they were some sort of weird licorice or something."

"Nope, they're Italian cigars, and old Vittorio smokes at least one or two of them a day. He breaks them in half and smokes half at a time. When he's smoked them down as far as he can, he butts them out and puts them in an old tin can. When he has enough saved up, he crushes them and rolls cigarettes with the tobacco."

By this time I was almost gagging at the thought. Just the smell of an ordinary cigar made me nauseous. My brother was clearly enjoying himself.

"That's not the end of it," he went on, "when he's smoked the rollies down as far as he can, he butts those out and puts them in another can. After he has a few saved up he squeezes the tobacco out into an old pipe and smokes that."

"Now that's just ridiculous," I said. "You're making this up, aren't you?"

"Swear to God," Ricky retorted, put out a bit by my skepticism. "I saw the can of cigarette butts myself, and Chris told me that was why he saved them. But wait, I'm not done yet. Chris told me that when Vittorio finishes smoking his pipe he scrapes the bowl out with his old pocket knife and puts the scrapings in his lip like our uncle Bert does with his Copenhagen snuff."

"That's just baloney. You're trying to make me sick," I said. "Nobody would do anything like that."

"Well," Ricky replied defensively, "I've been in his kitchen with Chris. I've seen the pipe and the knife, but I haven't seen a pouch or can of pipe to-bacco anywhere."

"So," I retorted, with obvious disgust in my voice, "that's your cigar story?"

"No, that's not it at all. I'm just telling you about Vittorio.

"A while back Chris and I were over to deliver some baking to him and he asked Chris if we would mind going down to Dobek's to get him half a dozen Roosters. That's what he calls those cigars for some reason. Vittorio doesn't like going down-town very much. He's just not really a social guy. He gave Chris a couple of bucks and told him he could keep the change."

"'Knowing my uncle, the change is not going to amount to much,' Chris told me as we headed off downtown.

"We got to Dobek's and Chris bought the six cigars and, surprisingly, there was a bit more money for us than he thought. Then Chris told the lady at the counter that since there was enough left over we would buy his uncle an extra cigar."

"I'm not so sure I really want to know where this whole thing is heading," I said, my rather weak protestation barely noted.

"Chris's uncle got his six cigars and we kept the seventh one for ourselves," my brother continued. "We swiped some matches from his house and we went down to Crazy Joe's to smoke it. It smelled pretty bad, even unlit.

"We ran into Steve and Perry, who were down there rafting and they wanted to join us. They gave us a ride on their raft out to the island so no one would spot us. Chris lit up, took a drag or two then started passing it around. At first, we were taking two or three drags each time we had our turn. Then it got down to one drag each. Finally, we stopped inhaling altogether and were just blowing the smoke out after every puff. I looked over at Chris and the others, and they all began looking seriously ill. I probably looked the same.

"I wanted to tell them that I'd had enough, but I didn't want to be the first one," Ricky admitted. "So all of us just kept right on smoking, hoping that one of the others would give it up. No one did."

"Why doesn't that surprise me?" I interjected, as Ricky continued rattling on.

"The cigar was down to less than two inches when Chris took it from me and it 'accidentally' dropped on the ground. We all stood there staring down at what we had now come to call the smoking dog turd. Chris looked around at the circle of us and asked, 'Anyone else want any more?' There wasn't a word spoken, and he crushed it into the wet grass with his heel.

"Every one of us was feeling terrible, but at least we were done and none of us faced the humiliation of being the first to quit. After all, who wants to suck on something that's been laying in the dirt, right?"

I just gazed in wonderment at my brother. No response was required. I thought about how this whole tale reminded me of some strange animal herd behavior I'd read about somewhere, but I couldn't quite put my finger on it.

We never said another word as we continued walking down the tracks, our heads down and our eyes intently glued to our steps in case we missed stepping on a tie and tripping. I had no idea why I was going down there with my brother in the first place. Maybe it was just to be with him.

A year or so later, when I discovered for sure that he was actually smoking pretty much full time along with most of his buddies, I just wondered, thinking back on the cigar story, "How on earth did that happen?"

Ricky had never related to me a single positive story that involved tobacco, yet there they were, all of them, all smoking. What could I expect, though? Back then it seemed that every adult smoked. Both of our parents certainly did, and even though most parents would counsel on the dangers of smoking to their kids—often with a cigarette in one hand—smoking was almost deemed a rite of passage. Stores could sell cigarettes to a ten-year-old and it wasn't an uncommon practice for parents to give their kids money and send them down to the store to fetch them a pack of smokes. Chris had gone into Dobek's and bought seven cigars, for god sake, with no questions asked.

Even though I personally had never taken a single puff on a cigarette, nor had I ever had the slightest urge to, I did have knowledge of tobacco uncharacteristic of my abstinence. Gratitude for that, once again, goes to my brother. Not all tobacco is smoked. I knew that from our uncle Bert who loved his Copenhagen snuff, a habit he'd gained from working as an underground miner.

Matt or Nick would often come over to the house to pick my brother up to go downtown for a pop at Fat's Café. Fat's was THE local hangout in Blairmore where you could often find your friends after school or on Saturday afternoons. This Saturday afternoon it was both of them that knocked on our back door.

It's funny how you get yourself attuned to certain things. If there was a knock on our back door and Rusty hadn't mounted a frenzy of barking, I just knew it had to be one of my brother's friends. Rusty knew and adored them all and his cute little cocker spaniel tail would wag uncontrollably at the sight of any of them. I guess he felt he was just another of the gang and his doggie heart would break every time he wasn't allowed to go with them, which happened only when they were headed somewhere that didn't allow dogs.

Matt had a dog, too, but you barely ever saw them out together. Ricky and Nick used to tease Matt that Shep was so ugly no one wanted to be seen out in public with him. He was arguably one of the homeliest bits of mangy meat, bone and hair ever to be mistakenly labeled a dog, according to my brother.

"Shep has this habit of sitting calmly on Matt's back step," he said. "Whenever we come through the back gate he just sits there passively until we get about halfway up the sidewalk to the house. Then he tears off the step; barking and snarling. He runs up to you like he's going to rip you to shreds unless you stand perfectly still and don't move a muscle. He only stops when Matt comes out and calls him off.

"Shep has never actually bit me," my brother continued. "But, none of us are going to test him on that.

"Now, whenever we go to Matt's place we just stand at the back fence and yell to him until he hears us and comes out. The strangest thing about Shep is that once we're all together and Matt's there with us he's a real jam tart. He even gets along well with Rusty."

"Well," I quipped, "Shep is probably just doing what he thinks is his job."

You're probably wondering right about now what all this has to do with anything. Nothing, really; I just tend to stray sometimes.

"Ricky's upstairs finishing off his monthly changing of the sheets and sweeping the dust bunnies out from under his bed," I said to Nick and Matt. "He's almost done. Do you want to wait in here for him or out on the back porch?"

They chose the latter as I knew they would. I called up to my brother and let him know his friends were waiting; then joined them on the porch. The first minute or so was a bit awkward for them since I don't think they expected my company.

Finally, Matt said, "Did Ricky happen to tell you about Tony and the chewing tobacco?"

"No," I replied, my curiosity immediately aroused. Nick gave Matt a reproachful look, like he should have kept his mouth shut, but the cat was already out of the bag.

Matt went on, "Yeah, we all chipped in for a plug of that Big Ben Chewing Tobacco last Saturday—Nick here, me, Ricky and Tony."

I knew by now that they all smoked, but chewing tobacco was taking it to a whole new level. The only guys that used that stuff were miners, and only, I presumed, because they couldn't smoke cigarettes underground.

"Oh, please," I said in mock earnestness, "Please, tell me more."

Appearing unaware of my blatant sarcasm, Matt continued. "We went over to the Pass Hotel lobby," he said. "And we all sat in those old chairs that are in there and Ricky unwrapped the plug. It looked a little like one of those Cuban Lunch chocolate bars, without the nuts."

"Uh, yes," I interjected. "The Pass Hotel lobby. Smart move. No chance of anyone seeing you there." This time I wasn't being flip.

It was true. The Pass Hotel lobby may well have gone down on record as being one of the most underutilized and lonely pieces of real estate in the entire town. Yes, the old oak chairs were still there, lined up along one wall, as was the counter, painted over six or seven times in the hotel's long and illustrious history. The registry book had long since disappeared, hardly a necessity any longer.

These were the days when liquor licenses were difficult, if not impossible, to get; the result of years of Alberta's deeply rooted, ultraconservative religious government. But virtually every one of the old small-town hotels historically had been granted a license to serve beer, and these hotels were regularly bought and sold on that basis alone; certainly not on the quantity nor quality of their guest rooms.

There was still a doorway from the lobby into the adjoining bar, but the only use it ever really got was the occasional old bachelor who wandered down from his room upstairs and went in for a beer or two. There were two other entrances: the main one on the front street, and Ladies and Escorts, discreetly tucked away around the corner on the side street. The hotel, like most others of its vintage, was built in the era when no self-respecting woman would be seen entering a bar unescorted lest she be labeled a shameless tramp, or worse.

The hotel had long since ceased to be a hotel in the conventional sense of it, but rather had a number of its rooms which rented by the month to older bachelors who didn't mind cooking their meals on a hot plate and using the common bathroom facilities down the hall.

"Ricky chewed off a small corner of the tobacco plug and passed it on to the rest of us," Matt continued. "We all took a small piece, chewed it up a bit and put it in our cheek like you're supposed to, but not Tony. No, he bit off a huge chunk; almost a third of the whole plug, chewed it all up and swallowed it. The three of us had each been spitting the tobacco juice into that white sand in the big ashtray and covering it up. Tony looked over at us, his normal dark Italian face turning a sickly, yellowish grey. He jumped out of his chair and headed for the door, but he didn't quite make it. He puked all the tobacco up right on the stairs, along with the twenty-five cent plate of sweet and sour rice he'd just ate at Fat's. We got out of the hotel right away, before anyone spotted us, and tossed the rest of the plug into a garbage can in the alley."

"Why do you guys do this kind of stuff?" I said to Matt, but just then my brother came through the back door and they were off. I didn't get my answer, but the question was largely rhetorical, anyway. Once again I was left with Rusty whining at our back gate with his big, sad eyes as the three went up the alley, jostling with one another as they always did.

Chapter 31

A Knee to The Ego

My brother didn't get into too many scraps in his younger days. In fact, short of the beating he took from the Grenier brothers, I can only remember him nursing one black eye from a fight. It wasn't because he was a sissy or anything like that. He was pretty wiry and tough and seemed to always come out on top when he was wrestling around on the lawn or in the park with his buddies.

What I really think is that Ricky found himself in what I would call a real sweet spot in terms of his reputation. Due to a few incidents in the neighborhood, he was known as a kid who wouldn't back away from a fight. By the same measure he wasn't one whose reputation inspired others to try and knock him off any perceived pedestal. That sort of thing was left to those really tough Simmons brothers from Hillcrest. All three of them had a well-earned reputation for fighting all the time, usually with those who thought they might be able

242

to successfully take them on. The Simmons boys weren't bullies, necessarily, but were the standard by which all other tough guys in the Pass measured themselves. And they were from Hillcrest, as well, which made the challenge even more enticing.

My brother came home one afternoon and he was worried. I could tell right away that something was eating at him.

"What's wrong," I asked.

"I just got in a fight with Robby," he replied. Robby Baratoli lived in the neighborhood, was a year older than my brother, and was one of the neighborhood's elites. He wasn't necessarily that tough, but he comported himself that way.

"How did that happen?" I questioned. "I thought you and Robbie were friends."

"We were up at the shale pit," Ricky said. "Robby and a few of his friends were pushing Matt and I around, sort of in fun. Robby and I started to wrestle a bit and he put me in a headlock. I got out of it and we started to push at one another. I thought at first it was all just fun, but after I squeezed out of his headlock he got really serious. Then, it was just him and I going at it. All the other guys were standing around watching us. He went to grab me by the head again. He didn't expect it, but I stepped in and kneed him right in the balls. He just dropped to his knees right there in front of me, holding his crotch and howling like a dog. I didn't know what to do, but I knew he was really pissed at me. I looked down at him for a second, then Matt and I decided we should just get the heck out of there."

"Robby can be a bit of a bully, alright," I said. "But you guys have hung around together for a long time. Maybe he'll just forget about it."

"I don't think so," Ricky replied. "Rob's cousin Larry and few other friends of his were there and saw what happened. I think he's going to want to get even, just to show them."

So my brother laid low for a few days and didn't venture too far into the neighborhood. To everyone's surprise, including his, nothing more ever came of it. Without a single word spoken, he and Robbie seemed to patch up any differences they might have had and things went on as usual. The ultimate outcome of it all, however, was that Ricky no longer endured any further bullying from any of the older guys. The same couldn't be said for a few of his other friends. Isn't it funny how that works?

Chapter 32

The Genesis of a Friendship

Though there were a few as time went on, just one other incident of my brother getting into an altercation comes to mind, only because its outcome was so baffling to me. We were in class one morning when the school's intercom came on with a message from the principal's office. "Will Ricky Callaghan and Roger Douglas please come to the principal's office?"

"Oh God," I thought, "What now?" Getting called down to the principal's office was never good news. It wasn't like you were being summoned there to have some sort of academic award bestowed upon you. It also didn't help that the school's intercom system meant that the entire student population knew you were in some sort of hot water.

I wiggled around restlessly in my desk for the rest of my math class, hardly able to contain my anxiety and unable to concentrate on anything going on in the classroom. If someone had asked me what three plus three was I would probably have been stumped.

At class break I rushed over to my brother's locker and waited for him to come out. When he approached from down the hall I asked him, perhaps a bit too hastily, "What happened?"

"Too long," he replied bluntly. "I'll tell you when we're going home for lunch." He exchanged his books and headed for his next class without another word.

It was another anxious hour for me until the noon buzzer went. As we walked together out the back entrance, I said, "Okay, now tell me."

"You know that new kid, Douglas?" Ricky started. I didn't, but that didn't matter.

"Everyone in the school does now," I replied. "I trust he can thank you for that."

"It wasn't all my fault," Ricky said defensively. "I was in the boys' can at our first class break taking a pee. Minding my own business. He came in and stood at the urinal next to me. We just looked at one another for the whole time we were doing our business and didn't say a word. Both of

246

us finished at about the same time, then turned to each other and began fighting. Just like that. He only started at school a few days ago and we haven't even spoken a word even though he's in class with me. He didn't start the fight and neither did I. It just started. It was like we both decided, at the same time, that we didn't like each other.

"Anyway, we were both getting at it pretty good. Not punching or anything serious like that, but both of us were trying to push the other guy's head into the urinal. A few guys came into the can and were just watching us go at it. We were pretty evenly matched actually, and after a while we both just got tired and stopped. By that time everyone in the hallway knew there was a fight going on in the washroom, including a few of the teachers, obviously, because it got back to the principal's office right away."

"So, what happened at the principal's office?" I asked.

"Not much," my brother replied. "We both got a real tongue lashing from Mr. Cernik. He told us he was going to report it to our parents, but I don't think he will, and he's making us do detention for the rest of the week."

"No strap, then?" I said, taking a quick glance down at my brother's hands.

"Nope, not this time," he grinned back at me.

One would think that that's where the story ends, but being that we're living in Ricky's world, that's far too simple. For the next four days both boys did their detention together in the school library, and with a certain disciplinary wisdom, both were seated across from each other at the same library table. It wasn't until the second day that they spoke their first words to each other. Then the dam broke loose.

"He's not a bad guy," Ricky said to me when he got home for supper after his second day of af-ter-class punishment. "Did you know that he's from Texas?" That fact alone seemed to impress my brother. "We're going to go down and do some rafting at Crazy Joe's this Saturday."

And with that rough and inexplicably strange start began one of the closest friendships of my brother's young life. It was a friendship that was to continue until the Douglas family moved on from Blairmore four years later. Ricky had never written a letter before in his life, but for a long time

after he and Roger Douglas carried on a steady cor-
respondence that eventually dwindled away as
time passed.

Chapter 33

The Chokerman

In our household, when you hit your teen years you could expect to be put to work in dad's sawmill, girls excluded, of course. Ricky was to be the last of the four boys in our family who would find himself with summer employment at Rocky Mountain Sawmills. He didn't mind. It was an opportunity to make some "real money", as he liked to put it.

Our dad was big on work ethic, and he made certain that all of the boys in the family acquired it whether they minded or not. But there was a real problem that dad had to wrestle with. On one hand he wanted his sons to adopt his own work ethic, but on the other, he prayed none of them would like the actual work itself and follow him into the lumber/sawmill business. He expected all of his children to seek higher education and move on to something more promising.

His solution was to give all of his boys, Ricky included, the crappiest, most menial jobs in the mill. Piling lumber off the green chain appeared to be his personal favorite, because if you liked doing that there was something seriously wrong with you, and you probably didn't deserve to go to college. But there were other gems as well like restacking lumber piles that had blown over in the wind or sorting mixed piles into separate stacks of common dimension. "Garbage jobs," as Ricky frequently referred to them as.

"Dad's doing the same thing to me at the mill that he did when he coached my Pee Wee hockey team when I was little," he complained to me.

"And what's that?" I asked.

"He's so damned scared of showing favoritism that he just goes out of his way to make sure he doesn't," he said with an unmistakable bitterness in his response. "I remember one game when he put me on the ice only once in each period, and I was the best forward on the team."

"I thought they had line changes in hockey?" I said.

"They do," he shot back, getting visibly angrier as our conversation went on, "but, dad would substitute my position with someone else almost every time. I didn't want to, but I ended up sitting in the corner of our players' box crying to myself."

"You were probably just imagining things," I consoled. "You know how competitive you can be."

"No," he replied. "I didn't imagine it. At the end of the game I overheard the coach on the other team chatting out in the lobby with dad, and he mentioned to him that he'd noticed I hadn't had much ice time. He asked if maybe I hadn't been feeling well.

Dad just said, 'No, he has to learn that he's not the star of the team.' I was seven years old, for Christ sake. I've never forgotten it, either," Ricky added. "I was glad when he stopped coaching. Now he's doing it to me all over again at the mill."

The mill would always need extra grunt laborers in the summer. That was the busy time in the lumber business. Dad would hire my brother and two or three of his friends for the seasonal work at the planer mill or out in the bush; always under the watchful eyes of his foremen. Though never admitted to, it would be a fair guess to assume that his foremen were advised, in no uncertain terms, not to show even the slightest hint of partiality towards his son. Certainly, my brother thought so, as did all three of our older brothers when they had worked for dad.

After a year or two of working in town at the big mill, Ricky got on with the bush crew at the company's Glacier Creek mill. The operation was a crazy assortment of characters including fallers, swampers, cat skinners, chokermen, scalers and buckers, sawyers, edgermen and other sundry laborers. Collectively they were a professional crew of skilled, competent lumbermen. Individually...well, that's another story.

"So, how was your first day in the bush?" I asked, tongue firmly in cheek when he came dragging his behind into the house just before supper.

"Why?" he replied curtly, noting my amused look. "You been talking to someone?"

"No'" I said. "Just curious, that's all. It was your first day on a 'real job'. Your words, remember?"

"Yeah, yeah," he mumbled. "I fell in the pond

this morning. You happy now? Thought you might have heard already. I was pretty much the laughing stock of the whole mill today."

"That couldn't have been so bad," I said. "So you got a little wet. Big deal. It was a hot day."

"You obviously haven't been to the Glacier Creek mill," he said irritably. "The log pond is fed by Glacier Creek. Let me say that again— 'Glacier' Creek! That's not just a name someone made up because they thought it sounded neat. The water coming into the pond is so damned cold you have to put it in a bottle and set it out in the sun for a while before you can even drink it. Otherwise, you get instant throat freeze.

"Tony, the foreman, thought working on the pond was the best place for me given it was my first day on the job and all. Pretty safe, too. All I had to do was make sure that the logs didn't get jammed up before they went on the feed chain and up to the head saw."

All of that sawmill lingo was Greek to me, but I sensed an interesting story coming, so I kept quiet and let him continue.

"I was catching on pretty quickly and doing really well. Probably getting a little careless, though.

I stabbed at a pretty small log with my pike pole. It stuck in the top of the log, but as soon as it did the log rolled over in the water. The tip of my pike pole came out. Then I lost my balance, tripped on the 2 by 4 along the edge of the catwalk and went into the water head first. The pond was deeper than I thought. I couldn't even touch bottom. Good thing I know how to swim, but it's not that easy with all of your work clothes on, including those heavy work boots.

"The rest of the landing crew was over on the other side of the pond, so it took them quite a while to get around to my side. I was holding onto the catwalk for dear life, and when the guys finally pulled me out I was so cold I could barely move and couldn't even speak. One of the guys told me my face had actually turned blue. They took me up to the diesel power shed and let me sit in there for two hours until I warmed up, stopped shaking and dried off a bit. Then it was back to the log pond for the rest of the afternoon. Dad will probably have them dock my wages for those two hours in the shed."

So that was day one in the bush for my brother. He stayed on the pond job for another week; then they put him out in the real bush as a chokerman.

He worked on a D-7 skid Cat with cat skinner, Willie Olin. Willy was someone I didn't know, but according to my brother he had a significant drinking problem.

"Willy reeks of stale booze every morning and his eyes are always bleary and bloodshot," Ricky said, "And I've never seen him smile."

He liked Willy, though. My brother had this thing for strange people that I would compare to the behavior of cats. You know what I mean; they always end up pestering the person in the room that likes them the least and ignoring everyone else.

The bush work must have been tough. I swear I could see my brother, physically at least, change from a boy to a man in those few months. I wasn't sure it was for the better, or that I liked it. Just life, I guess. I was kind of missing my 'little brother'.

"What exactly does a chokerman do?" I asked him one evening as we were sitting out on the back lawn in the two old Adirondack chairs; the ones that dad had built himself and painted up to match the two-tone paint on the house siding. Ricky was busy rubbing Noxzema from a big blue jar on his scratched, scraped and bug-bitten legs and arms. Mom firmly believed Noxzema healed everything, and it had been a staple in our medicine cabinet for as long as I could remember: Noxzema and Vaseline.

"The job's sort of hard to explain," he said. "But I'll try and keep it simple. I'm the guy who ties the fallen trees to the winch on the Cat so we can drag them out of the bush and down to the landing. From the landing they're loaded up and trucked to the mill. It's probably the shittiest job in the bush. I mean, look at my legs and arms. They look like they've been through a meat grinder.

"I don't even want to wear my shorts or my swimming suit this summer. My hands are always sore from being jabbed with spines from those steel choker cables. Look at them. They're a mess. But the worst are those tiny little black flies. They drive you crazy. I have to tie the bottoms of my pants up with binder twine so they don't get up my legs, but they still do, anyway.

"Even if it's eighty-five degrees out there you don't dare take off your shirt or even roll up your sleeves. They bite like crazy and they get up your nose and in your eyes. When they get really bad we have to rub diesel fuel on ourselves. That seems to keep them away for a while anyway. But the diesel smells terrible and I can still smell it on me, even after a bath.

"Why don't you just ask mom for some bug repellent?" I asked innocently.

"I thought about that," Ricky replied, "But all the older guys told me not to bother. It doesn't work with those little bastards."

I'd noticed my brother's language skills were definitely taking a marked downturn since he'd begun working in the bush.

"It's the worst job I've ever had," he confessed, which was strange coming from my brother, because for all of his other faults he'd never shied away from hard work.

"I don't know who they get to do it in the wintertime," he added, "but at least they don't have to put up with the bugs."

"Why don't you just ask dad to put you on another job?" I said.

He looked me straight in the eye, feigning something that wasn't quite resignation, and said, "You have got to be kidding! And admit to dad that the job is too tough for me?"

I felt a little sorry for my brother then, because he was genuinely distressed. But then, right as I was feeling the worst for him, there it was, that crazy little crooked smile of his.

"What?" I said. "You tell me this tale of misery, get me feeling all sorry for you, then you smile. Are you some kind of nut case?"

"No, I was just thinking," he said, "at least I've got Willy. He may reek of stale wine every day, but our bush boss did put me with the best cat skinner."

The smile told me I was in for another of my brother's great tales.

"Billy Daniels is working as a chokerman on the other Cat. He got put with Johnny Marshall," he started in, as if I was just supposed to understand the significance of that.

Billy was another of my brother's close friends and his dad also worked in the sawmill, so it was no real coincidence that the two found themselves working at the same jobs in the bush but on two different skid crews. "What's wrong with Johnny Marshall?" I asked, pretending that I actually knew the guy.

"Well, nothing really, other than I found out from Billy that Johnny has a really strange heart condition. He can fall asleep in an instant, for no reason," said Ricky.

"Both crews were having lunch together last Friday. That doesn't happen very often, but last week we were working close together. Anyway, Johnny was just about to take a bite of his sandwich. He had it right up to his mouth and he fell sound asleep, just like that. He didn't even drop the sandwich. He stayed that way for about half a minute or so, then he woke right up and finished eating, like nothing had even happened.

"It was pretty weird. I hadn't seen him do that before, but everybody else on the regular bush crew seemed to know all about his condition. They just kept right on chatting and eating like nothing had happened, while Johnny sat there taking his little catnap.

"Anyway, that's not the worst of it," my brother went on. "Earlier this week Billy was sitting on the armrest of the Cat as Johnny was driving it back into the timber block for another load. Johnny fell asleep. The Cat hit a big tree stump and the impact threw Billy right off the Cat and into the deadfall beside the skid road. He only scratched himself up a bit, but it sure scared the shit out of him. Since then he's refused to get back on the Cat and walks behind it, in and out, all day. By the end of the shift the poor guy is dead tired. The work is rough enough as it is without having to do all that walking, too.

"Billy mentioned the incident to the bush foreman," my brother continued. "But, all he was told was that chokermen aren't really supposed to be riding on the Cats in the first place, something about Workers' Compensation rules. I guess cat skinners are hard to come by so they're a little more valuable than chokermen. Anyway, I'm glad I've got Willy even though he stinks and doesn't talk much."

"You should really be telling dad about this," I said.

"Not really any of my business," said Ricky laconically. "At the end of August I'm out of there and back to school. I'm not going back in the bush next summer, and I don't think I want to work for dad anymore, either."

And he didn't.

Chapter 34

Recollections

I remember the weekend like it was yesterday. It was early August. I recall it so clearly because it was the first weekend in my life that I was to spend all alone. It wasn't as though I'd never been by myself before, but this was going to be different. Two full days completely on my own. Mom and dad had gone off to B.C. with three other couples on a golfing runaway, something they had never done before. Ricky was at some weekend youth camp down around Waterton with the United Church teen club he and his friends had joined. All of our older siblings were long gone, and for the past few years it had only been Ricky and me.

Everyone had said their good-byes and had all departed late Friday afternoon. The freezer compartment in the fridge was stocked with those new-fangled frozen T.V. dinners that mom had bought for me. There were two roast beef and one turkey dinner, and I chose the latter because of the applesauce dessert. Half an hour in the oven and "voila", dinner was ready. I could get used to these T.V. dinners, I thought, after tossing the tinfoil plate into the trash, leaving only a knife and fork to wash up.

Then, I went into the living room and watched T.V. for a few hours. I turned it off after the CBC News and went upstairs to my room. I had thought of calling Marlene and chatting for a while, but it was already getting late and I knew her parents wouldn't appreciate it. Besides, she was probably out on a date with her new boyfriend, Charles, or Chucky as I liked to call him. Marlene wasn't fond of the nickname I'd chosen for her new paramour, but I didn't care. I was trying to protect her. Chucky was actually pretty good looking and I thought that if I could make him at least sound like a dork, it might lessen Marlene's attraction to him. That turned out to be a futile effort.

It wasn't as though our family was raucous and noisy all the time like some of those Italian families in the neighborhood, but the silence of being alone with no other people noises was something unnaturally disquieting to me. I sat on my bed with my back up against the headboard and tried to start reading a new novel I'd picked up at the library the day before. At any other time, I would have probably dug right in, but tonight my brain was all over the place and my ability to concentrate had left me. It was like I had to do something, but I didn't know what. I put down the book and my eyes wandered aimlessly around my room. It had been mine for the last several years after Paula had finished high school and left for Calgary. It had always been designated the girls' room because, unlike the other upstairs bedrooms, it had a door.

I got off my bed and wandered, for no apparent reason, into my brother's bedroom. The stinky sock smell, as usual, assaulted my senses and the whole room had that distinct "a teenage boy lives here" aura about it, but tonight, for some reason, it was oddly comforting. I made a mental note to myself not to be as hard on Ricky about his personal hygiene as I had been. At the same time, I doubted I'd have the intestinal fortitude to follow that through in any significant way.

I went over to his dormer window and slid it open to let some much-needed fresh air into the room. The dead flies that had met their end stuck in small puddles of airplane model glue were still there, lined up on the wide windowsill, their dried up corpses testament to the childhood cruelty that my brother and his friends had gotten up to.

I didn't know why I was wandering aimlessly around like some ghost in an attic, so I returned to my own bedroom. I closed the door, though I didn't need to, and determined to sleep. The last time I checked the alarm clock on my bedside table its luminous hands said it was 1:45 a.m. I must have finally drifted off sometime after that.

Marlene came over the next morning and I was glad for her visit even though I was a bit tired and cranky. It seemed I was not the loner I thought I was. As I'd correctly guessed, my best friend had been out with Chucky the night before.

"It was just our second date, and he's so, so much fun," Marlene said in her typical dramatic fashion. It was the second "so" that cinched it for me. She was head over heels in love... yet again.

"I guess I could go back to calling him Charles," I thought to myself. "I've clearly lost this one."

Marlene babbled on, "We got back to my house and sat in his dad's car for quite a while and I let him kiss me, Frenchy-style. He tried to, y'know, feel me up a bit, but I didn't let him. Maybe next time, but only on top." Marlene looked at me like she expected I should bestow the Medal of Virtue on her, but I just decided to keep my mouth shut and let her rattle on.

"So, what you up to tonight?" she asked. "Folks are away; let's have a party here."

She didn't miss the look I shot back at her, then smiled, jostled me gently on the shoulder and said, "Just kiddin', Pooh Pooh. Lighten up."

Marlene was the only person who ever called me that and only when it was just the two of us together. It was the nickname she used only when I wasn't buying into one of her countless hare-brained schemes. She knew I didn't like it, but strangely enough it was one of those intimately shared things that bound us together. I was never able to come up with a nickname for her that would adequately put us on a level playing field—not without the risk of seriously hurting her feelings.

"You weren't calling me Pooh Pooh last summer when you spent those two weeks crying on my shoulder because you'd missed your period," I reminded her.

"Yeah, well that was different," she shot back.

"I was really scared that I was up the stump. Thank God it turned out to be a false alarm. You don't have to remind me of that, either."

"Well," I said, "It should be a reminder to you to make sure that Chucky there keeps his hands and his other appendage well above your waist."

"You're always using those big words," she whined. "Always trying to make me feel uneducated. What's an appendage?"

"Oh nothing," I said, knowing that she'd already missed my point and not entirely certain she wasn't just playing me. Marlene was impetuous, for sure, but she wasn't stupid. She reminded me so much of my younger brother it was scary. She was just a slightly older, female version. It caused me to wonder why it was that close friendships, more often than not, involve polar opposites. Most of my other friends were just like me, but Marlene... well, let's just say she wasn't, and leave it at that.

She left after an hour and we agreed to meet after supper, go for a pop at Fat's and take in a movie. Then I embarked on a quest that I'd set my mind to the night before; one that I'd had in the

back of my mind ever since I took over the bedroom from Paula when she left home six years before. Today was the day, the very first day, that I
knew I would be able to do it, completely uninter-
rupted.

The history of the upstairs of our home had always been a bit of an unknown. At one end of my
bedroom there was an old, built-in kitchen vanity
with a well-worn white enameled metal sink still
set into the countertop, which was finished in some
sort of ancient red linoleum and trimmed with
chrome. It was obvious that at some point in its
life, our upstairs had been used as a bachelor suite.
Even before we moved in all of the plumbing to the
sink had been disconnected and removed. The vanity immediately became the storage place for the
family's two big Carnation canned milk boxes of
photos, several albums and other assorted family
memorabilia. The sink itself held a Monopoly
Game, a Milles Borne card game and two or three
jigsaw puzzles. I kept some of my personal things
on the countertop as well.

But, underneath... that's where the real mystery lay. Oddly, though, it shouldn't have been so.
None of us had ever really been forbidden to look
or browse through the cupboard's contents. Had

they held some deep, dark family secrets our parents certainly wouldn't have chosen to put them there available to the prying eyes of six nosy offspring. No, it was just ignored in an inexplicable, almost fearful manner by all of us. It was the damnedest thing.

As I opened the two front cupboard doors I could feel my heart beating faster. "This is crazy," I said to myself out loud. I wasn't doing anything I shouldn't be doing, but somehow it didn't feel that way.

I reached in and grabbed a pile off the top that included loose papers, some old brochures and a few thin booklets. They were obviously things not valuable enough for my parents to have put away in a box or even a folder. I put them on the floor and sorted through what was there. The only things that really caught my eye were the two booklets with their sickly, faded pastel green covers. They were Canadian Army issue pieces on the horrors of venereal disease, designed doubtlessly to scare the living bejeezuz out of any soldier considering having unprotected sex. They were probably my dad's, since he had served in the army during World War II. The photo illustrations in both booklets were beyond ghastly, particularly the one dealing with syphilis. There were horribly graphic images of men with half of their genitals rotted off while others showed huge oozing sores and blisters on various parts of the body, including the face. Over my disgust I managed the rather wicked thought of showing the booklet to Marlene to steer her off her course of growing promiscuity.

Then, it was on to those big, thick albums. I hadn't planned to even touch either of the two big boxes of photos. There simply wouldn't be enough time in the whole weekend.

The first big album I opened turned out to be pure gold. There, right on page one was a big ten by eight-inch picture of mom and dad's wedding party. I recognized my parents right away, but I knew none of the others except one older fellow who looked a little like mom, probably one of my uncles whom I had never met. My eyes strayed down to the bottom of the picture, and there it was, neatly written in pen, my mom and dad's names and under that the date. I did some quick math in my head. It was, almost to the day, five months before my own birthday. I looked at the picture for a second time and noticed just the slightest trace of a baby bump on my mother's tailored dress, a slight bulge that might otherwise have gone unnoticed.

"There I am, that's me," I said quietly to myself. "Little wonder they haven't ever celebrated their wedding anniversary."

But that was it. There was no more. I paged through the rest of the album and there were no pictures of me. There were several that included the older kids in our family with and without mom and dad. I thought that maybe it was just the fashion of the day not to take baby pictures.

The second album contained photos of my dad in the army and a few other real cool ones with him and some of his friends, probably in the late 1930s, all suited up and walking down some busy street in Vancouver. There were others of him and his friends swimming at a lake somewhere.

The third album at the bottom of the pile was obviously the newest of the three given its appearance. On the front if it was a hand-printed label that read simply, "A New Start." I opened it to discover that it was a photo history of our family's move from the coast to Alberta. Mom and dad had obviously decided to make a vacation of the move and had taken tons of pictures. The album included photos of our family crossing over from Vancouver

Island on the ferry, various stops at restaurants and roadside attractions along the way: a stay-over at some lake resort, and our eventual arrival in the Crowsnest Pass. There they were--mom, dad, my older half-siblings and even my little brother, Ricky, just a tyke at the time. I looked through the album front to back a second time now completely bewildered. Had I missed some pages? No, I hadn't I concluded after the third time through.

There was no "me"

Kathryn

Two Truths

It was early spring. Buds were beginning to form on the trees in the yard, and the morning had started wonderfully—pleasantly warm and sunny. It should have been one of those days when you simply threw back your arms and breathed it all in and reveled in the knowledge that you had made it through another long, cold mountain winter.

Elizabeth felt none of that. Deep inside her dwelled the knowledge that she was truly alone. It had begun just after the New Year. She had chalked it up to a simple case of seasonal melancholy, not foreign to her since she had suffered it for years now. But it was somehow different this time. Yes, Ernest was there, as he'd always been, but her mind wandered to the vague recollection of Kathryn going off to business school in Calgary last fall, and Ricky having that big blow up with his father over his poor school performance.

They both had packed up and moved out at almost the same time. Ricky had gone to Calgary, too, moved in with Kathryn and found a job working at his Uncle Al's car dealership there. Mr. Bannon had phoned her and Ernie when Ricky had arrived at his office looking for work just to make sure everything was okay with them. It really wasn't, but they were relieved to know that there would be some oversight and that their youngest would at least have one adult close by should the need ever arise. He wasn't one quite yet himself.

Ricky hadn't been back since leaving, sending a clear message in his own stubborn way that he was going to make it on his own and did not require any further parental guidance in his life. Kathryn had been home for Christmas, but the visit was brief and cloaked in a strange, puzzling tension. She and her mom had barely spoken, almost as though their relationship had come to some awkward conclusion. Elizabeth felt an emotional duality about the situation that felt completely foreign to her. She had said goodbye to her daughter and by that same circumstance had gained a rather disconcerting personal freedom, a freedom she hadn't been prepared to deal with.

The truth was, Elizabeth's life had plummeted,

and the ennui she was feeling seemed unshakeable. But it was a warm spring day and not much had been done around the house for a good long time. She felt that a day of spring housecleaning might just be the elixir she needed to get through her numbing despondency.

Some of the upstairs closets were now beginning to take on that odor of dust-shrouded mustiness that accompanies the stillness of disuse. Elizabeth was by no means a poor housekeeper. Quite the contrary, but the boxes, the books, and the old, outdated clothing that occupied many of these closets were saddening memories of times long-since past. They were happier times, perhaps, and happy memories—if you were anyone but Elizabeth Callaghan. She drew a deep breath and opened the first closet; the one in the hallway between the bedrooms, two large cardboard boxes at the ready for she knew the time had finally come to de-clutter both her home and her mind.

A stack of old clothes piled on the closet floor caught her eye first, some carelessly discarded there, others that had slipped to the floor after being hastily hung above on an assortment of old wire hangers. Elizabeth grabbed them up like one of those digger games at a summer midway, and stuffed the handful into the waiting cardboard box not bothering to sort through any of it. As she went for a second scoop she noticed the corner of a burgundy hardbound journal sticking out from the remaining pile. She was certain she felt her heart stop for just a brief second. It was Kathryn's. Her name had been etched in black grease pencil on the front cover.

Elizabeth, prone to inquisitiveness only in the most motherly of ways, thumbed through the first five or six pages of the journal, her pulse quickening as she read.

* * *

The phone rang three times at Dr. Stanley Harding's office. Then Elizabeth heard the familiar voice of Ella, his receptionist. Elizabeth and Ella were about the same age, and typical of a small town, they were friends who shared a number of common interests, like curling, golf and the Legion Ladies Auxiliary. Dr. Harding had been the Callaghan family doctor ever since they had moved to Blairmore, and Ella had been his receptionist for even longer. Her longevity was due, in no small part, to her ability to keep a confidence, and in a small town like Blairmore that was an asset valued far beyond those mundane and readily acquired skills like typing and record keeping.

"What's up, Elizabeth?" she said, in that informal fashion she reserved for those she knew best.

"Oh, I'd just like to make an appointment with Dr. Harding as soon as possible," Elizabeth responded, trying to keep her reply as casual and informal as possible. Anticipating what Ella's next question would be, Elizabeth volunteered, "It's just a personal matter that I think Dr. Harding may be able to help me with."

"Let's see. How does tomorrow 1:30 sound?" Ella offered. "Dr. Harding's just had a cancellation."

"That would be great. Thanks, Ella. I'll see you tomorrow afternoon," Elizabeth replied, mustering all the unfelt enthusiasm she could. She hung up the phone, went back upstairs and continued to page through the journal.

Housework had been forgotten and Elizabeth sat on the edge of Kathryn's now-abandoned bed and leafed through the journal from front to back. Tears streamed down her face uncontrollably and she just let them soak into her apron. She felt convulsive pains grip her chest, relieved only by letting go of any emotional constraint she might have felt necessary.

When she had cried all she could, she carefully placed the journal aside and continued to sit at the edge of her daughter's bed. She felt sadness for what she'd just read, but it was accompanied by a mysterious peace as well. The depression she had fought for so long seemed, at least for the moment, partially lifted from her.

Ernie would be coming home from work in a few hours. Elizabeth went back downstairs and bathed her face in cold water until her tear-reddened eyes returned almost to normal. By the time Ernie got home all traces would be gone. Over the years she had learned to protect the man she loved so dearly from sharing her personal demons. He loved her and she him, and that was that. She didn't feel any need to burden him with her personal problems, so she had locked them away where no one, especially her husband, could find them.

When Ernie got home from work he changed from his sawmill work clothes, cleaned up, and by the time he got to the kitchen table Elizabeth had two rye and water highballs ready. They'd had this routine for years and supper had never started before they had had their one single drink and talked about their day. Neither of them were heavy drinkers, but this one-on-one time they shared was one of the bricks in their solid marriage.

Elizabeth talked about her spring housecleaning but neglected to mention anything of the journal she had discovered. Ernie sensed something different about his wife tonight, although he couldn't quite put his finger on it. He wasn't a terribly sensitive person in the classic sense of it, but under his rough exterior and his famous temper was a man whose sentimentality could be almost embarrassing, given the hard-assed persona he had crafted for himself. He had a soft spot for all women, and he loved and adored Elizabeth.

In a rare and uncharacteristic reminiscence, Ernie confided to friends at a small house party to the moment he had truly fallen in love with her. In his younger years he had been a scrapper; that being forced upon him having grown up in Vancouver's waterfront area, the middle child in a Black Irish family that included two older, bigger and meaner brothers. In those days Vancouver was also a very rough port city with few friendly suburbs. Topping up at just over five foot five, he could not be characterized as a big bruiser. But he was tough and had even done a short stint as a boxing prizefighter in a few of the city's seedier fight venues, something he never talked about.

"Liz and I were at a dance," he recounted, third or fourth beer in hand and looking over, love-eyed at her, not quite sure now that he should be telling the story. "We'd just started seeing one another and this was about our fourth or fifth date.

"There was a group of single guys there who were a bit drunk and started hassling some of the others who were there with their wives or girlfriends. Two of them came up to us on the dance floor and one of them tried to butt in," Ernie continued. "He gave me a push and that's when the fists started to fly. I was getting the upper hand with him, but then his pal decided he was going to step in and improve their odds. That's when Liz took off one of her high heels, picked it up like it was a hammer, stepped in front of him and told him that if he took one more step she was going to plant the heel right between his eyes. That stopped him dead in his tracks. I knocked the guy down that I was fighting with, then the whole thing came to an end. The two guys and their other friends were hustled out of the dance hall."

To some, characterizing this a "love story"

would be a bit of a stretch, but for Elizabeth and Ernie it was much more than just another fistfight at a dance hall. It was the moment that put form to their relationship. It defined the foundation upon which both of them, particularly Elizabeth, planned building a new family and their future together.

Elizabeth was right on time for her 1:30 appointment with Dr. Harding. Ella was the very personification of discretion, but nonetheless, Elizabeth wanted to minimize the time spent in the waiting room and possibly having to explain the contents of the large, brown paper shopping bag that she carried in with her. Not that it mattered to Ella, but Elizabeth felt the need to avoid any unnecessary conversation about it and she hadn't prepared for any sort of subterfuge.

"Dr. Harding is just back from lunch and has had a few phone calls to return," Ella explained. "He'll be with you in a minute or two. I've already given him all your charts."

Elizabeth caught herself before saying, "Oh, they won't be necessary," but thought the better of it. This was, after all, not really to do with her. She sat nervously for the next few minutes and leafed through a dog-eared old copy of Redbook magazine that was sitting on the arborite coffee table with several others in similar condition. The magazine didn't really interest her. She just wanted to avoid further conversation with Ella. Any other time and under any other circumstance, the two of them would probably be chatting up a storm about the women's golf league or the Legion Ladies upcoming spring bake sale. Today, Elizabeth just felt vulnerable and guarded and didn't quite know why, so it was a relief to her when Dr. Harding appeared in the doorway of his examining room.

"Come on in, Liz," he said as he caught her attention. He gave her a warm hug as she edged past him and entered.

This was why she and Ernie had kept Dr. Harding, or 'Stan', as everyone called him outside of work, as their family physician for all these years. There were two other doctors in town, but neither of them was quite as warm and caring as Dr. Harding. Over the years the relationship had grown to one of deep friendship. Dr. Harding had that rare quality of being able to keep his personal and social life separate from his medical practice.

It was one of the reasons Ella had been with

him for so long. She understood the delicate balance that his profession demanded and why he treated her more as a partner than an employee. He was the only person Liz felt comfortable discussing her most intimate concerns with, and there had been a few over the years. It was Dr. Harding who had advised her that it would be extremely unsafe for her to have any more children. And it was he who four months later, performed the necessary operation that ensured that it wouldn't happen by accident.

The family had never been religious, so ministerial guidance was most certainly not an option. This was the first time Elizabeth had sought Dr. Harding's advice on a matter that had little or no medical connection.

She sat down in the chrome and vinyl padded armchair with her package held guardedly on her lap. Dr. Harding sat close to her in a similar chair opposite and away from his examining bench with its telltale chrome stirrups. Elizabeth liked that he didn't choose to sit behind his old oak desk. That always seemed an emotional barrier to her, like going to the bank for a loan. Dr. Harding wasn't like that.

"How have you been, Liz?" he asked. "We haven't seen you in here for over a year since you caught that nasty ear infection." At the same time, he glanced down at the package on Elizabeth's lap and went on, with a smile and a quick wink, "And it looks like you brought me a present this time."

Elizabeth knew it was his tactful and instinctive way of opening the conversation without coming right out and saying, "What can I do for you today?" Why else would anyone walk into a doctor's office with a brown paper bag if it didn't have something to do with the visit?

"I've been fine," she replied. "A little bit of spring fever, that's all. You know how I get when the seasons change."

There was a short, knowing pause, then she went on, "This isn't about me, actually." She glanced down at the package on her lap and continued, "I've got something here that I'd like you to take a look at. I found it in an old closet upstairs in the house when I was doing some cleaning yesterday."

As she spoke, Dr. Harding could immediately sense an eerie difference in Elizabeth's demeanor. He could almost feel a veil drop down between them, the familiarity they always shared had somehow, inexplicably drifted away. It perplexed him, and it felt as though he were meeting a new patient for the first time. He sensed something was seriously wrong here, and he also knew that the answer was likely in that package on her lap.

Elizabeth opened the bag and drew out the thick, burgundy journal. She said nothing as she handed it across to her doctor.

He took it, placed it on his lap and said, "What is this?"

"I need you to read it," Elizabeth replied, deepening the mystery. "Not all of it, of course, but at least some of it. Then we can talk."

Dr. Harding turned the book over, opened it to its first page and did as she requested. Half a minute in and with half the first page read, he felt his body tensing. Something was profoundly wrong here. All of his professional senses told him to proceed with caution, and he hoped Elizabeth had not noticed the change in him. He read three more pages as Elizabeth sat patiently waiting.

He closed the book, set it gently on his side table and looked directly at Elizabeth without saying a word.

"It's Kathryn's," Elizabeth said finally. "She must have forgotten it and left it behind when she moved to Calgary. I'd never seen it before yesterday. It's some sort of diary or journal that she's had for God knows how long."

Dr. Harding sat silently letting Elizabeth proceed unprompted.

"As you know, Kathryn's not living at home anymore," she continued. "But, I'm still her mother and I'm concerned for her."

There was another awkward silence.

"She's always been, you know, quiet and kept to herself a lot. I used to hear her quite often up in her bedroom talking to herself, but all kids do that, don't they?

"Yeah, they do," Dr. Harding mumbled in agreement, distracted slightly by his own thoughts. "But they do all sorts of strange things, Liz. You should know, you've raised a few in your day. Kids deal with things such as loneliness and isolation in any number of ways. It's not necessarily good or bad, it just 'is', and they usually grow out of it."

Dr. Harding was doing his best to maintain his professional composure.

"Can you leave this with me for a week or two?" he asked, placing his hand on the journal. "I'd really like to take the time to read it right through. Then we can talk again. Maybe we can get Ernie in on the conversation, too."

"No, no, that's not necessary," Elizabeth replied in a feeble attempt at nonchalance. "He's up to his ears with things at the mill and I don't really want to bother him with this. It's probably nothing, anyway."

"Alright," Dr. Harding replied as Elizabeth stood up to leave. "I'll have Ella call you in a week or so and set up a time."

"Thank you, doctor," she said as she turned to leave, giving him a quick hug. For the briefest moment Dr. Harding saw the old Elizabeth that he knew so well return in her eyes. Strange, indeed.

Dr. Harding had a half hour to spare before driving over to make the daily rounds with his patients at the hospital. Not knowing the nature of Elizabeth's concerns, he had asked Ella to pencil in more time than it had actually taken. That was okay. He needed the time to think and to read through the rest of the journal Elizabeth had left in his care, including a few loose, folded pages tucked into the pocket inside its front cover. He called out to Ella to hold any calls.

This was going to be a tough one, and he needed time to consider how he was going to deal with it. He'd known Elizabeth and Ernie it seemed like forever. He didn't know of another couple that he could say were as solid as these two were. They'd been through the trials of blending their families, which was no small challenge, and had come out stronger and closer for it. They'd had more than their share of adversity and had won out, always as a couple. Though he knew Ernie's temper was more bluster than substance, Dr. Harding had always admired Elizabeth's quiet way of handling it, always with her subtle dignity and strength. He knew she had all the tricks to bring him to bay. For certain, she struggled with her depression, but Dr. Harding had never considered it to be a debilitating condition. He couldn't imagine how wrong he'd been.

Had Elizabeth and Ernie been any other couple, Dr. Harding would not have felt the ethical conflict he was experiencing right at this moment. He knew in his heart that the decision he was about to make was the right one. He also knew there would be no turning back.

Looking through his desktop phone directory he found Ernie's business number at the sawmill. He picked up the phone and with no further hesitation called the number. After three or four rings, Ernie picked up and answered.

"Ernie, this is Dr. Harding. I don't want to startle you, but I was hoping that you might be able to drop into my office in the next day or so. I need to talk to you about a few things. I don't like to keep you in the dark and it's certainly not life or death, but it's also not something we can deal with over the phone."

Ernie was startled by the call, but at the same time was calmed by his doctor's caution that it was not cause for undue trepidation. He had always trusted his doctor's good judgment and knew he never acted rashly.

"I can make it over there tomorrow afternoon, if that works for you," he replied.

"I'll have Ella make the appointment for 2:00 o'clock tomorrow, then. One more thing, Ernie, please don't mention a word of this to Elizabeth. You'll understand when we meet."

Dr. Harding hung up the phone. He'd just done

something he never done in his entire medical career. The irreversible decision he had just made left him with an unsettling mix of anxiety and dread.

Then he let Ella know that Ernie Callaghan would be coming in tomorrow at 2:00 and to allow at least an hour on his appointment calendar. If Ella was confused she never let on.

Ernie stewed over the unexpected phone call for the rest of the afternoon. In the absence of any information, his imagination gravitated to the direst of possible circumstances. Was Elizabeth ill? Did she have some ghastly and incurable medical condition?

No, he thought, it couldn't be that. Dr. Harding had softened the shock of his unexpected call with his calming counsel against undue alarm. And yet... why the urgency?

That night he didn't sleep well and had wished that he'd made the appointment for the morning, rather than afternoon. He woke up cranky and irritable but did his best to hide it from Elizabeth. The morning at work dragged on seemingly forever, and for each hour his tension grew. After a few unwarranted explosions, those unfortunate enough to be working with him that morning began giving him a wide berth.

At lunch Ernie remained sullen and uncommunicative, lost in his thoughts.

He arrived at Dr. Harding's office ten minutes before two.

"Hi, Ernie. Dr. Harding will be out in a minute," Ella greeted him. The phone on her desk rang and she picked it up, nodded a few times and put it back down.

"Dr. Harding says to just go right in," she said. "He's been waiting for you."

"I'll bet not nearly as badly as I've been waiting for him," Ernie thought to himself.

Today, Dr. Harding chose to sit behind his desk. For some reason he felt the gravitas of the situation that he was about to discuss with Ernie required this extra layer of formality. The burgundy journal was sitting on his desk to one side in preparation for this meeting.

He stood up as Ernie entered the room, reached across the desk and offered a handshake. For both of them the air of formality felt a little stilted, since the two of them had been close personal friends for years. Ernie had always respected the air of friendly formality his doctor always assumed in his responsibility as such. The duality of it always left Ernie assured that anything discussed in his doctor's office was sure to remain totally confidential. On the golf course they were both very different people.

Today, though, the formality he'd come to know felt much different and Ernie picked up on it immediately. He sensed the presence of a very real tension the moment he stepped into the examining room and had a feeling that this meeting was going to be quite unlike any he'd had previously with his doctor. He sat nervously in one of the two chairs in front of the big antique desk.

"I'm sorry for all the cloak and dagger stuff yesterday, Ernie," Dr. Harding started. "It certainly wasn't my intent to scare the wits out of you. I can tell from the look on your face that I failed in that regard," he added in a small attempt at humor. "I've unfortunately found myself in a situation that, frankly, has me quite uncomfortable, but I am confident that I have made the right decision in the long run."

"Has this got to do with Elizabeth in any way?" Ernie asked, anxious to get to the meat of things, while at the same time trying to mask the impatience that had been building since the previous day.

"Yes, it does," Dr. Harding replied, "And that is exactly the conundrum I find myself in. But, before we go any further with this, I need you to take a look at the journal that Elizabeth brought in and left with me yesterday. I read through the whole thing after she left my office and before I called you."

He pushed the book across the desk to Ernie. He was somewhat confused, but followed his doctor's request. He sat there, a look of increasing bewilderment showing on his face as he went through the first few pages. Dr. Harding could not help noticing the color leaving Ernie's face as he read on.

Looking up and straight into his doctor's eyes, with a stunned look that Dr. Harding had never seen on him before Ernie said, "What does this mean, Stan?"

Suddenly, to Ernie, this was no longer a meeting to discuss a medical matter, and any pretense of professional decorum was dropped.

Dr. Harding was momentarily confused by this obvious change up, but immediately understood that Ernie was reaching out for more than just medical advice. He also needed a friend to interpret it for him.

"I think you know what it means, Ernie," he answered, "But, there's more here that we need to discuss. I want you to know before we continue, however, that I am seriously compromising my professional ethics by doing so, and could actually lose my license to practice medicine. I've thought long and hard about it, and have come to the conclusion that what I am doing here is the best course of action, professionally and personally, and worth that risk.

"Shall I go on?"

"Yes," Ernie replied.

"When Elizabeth brought me this journal yesterday, she asked me to take a look at it, just as I had asked you to do a few moments ago. Something was wrong, and I realized it the moment I read the first page.

"I took the time to read a few more pages in order to gather my thoughts. Putting the book aside, I looked straight at Elizabeth and just let her talk. The first thing she said to me was that she felt Kathryn might be having some sort of mental or emotional issues.

"I didn't know what to say at that point so I just let her go on about it, which she did for another few minutes. The thing that really struck me was Elizabeth herself. She had a very mysterious, unsettling look about her. I can't quite explain it. It wasn't as though she was in a trance or anything like that. It's just that it wasn't the Elizabeth I've come to know over the years."

"What are you saying?" Ernie choked out, his voice catching with nervousness.

"We both know there is no Kathryn, Ernie. She died in the Campbell River General Hospital three days after she was born. I've got copies of all that in my files, including her death certificate. You brought all that stuff in to me when your family first moved here.

"As for Ricky, well, we all know about him and the train."

There was a long pause. Neither of them spoke and neither could look directly at each other for a very long moment.

Finally, Ernie repeated, "What are you saying?" This time the question took on considerably more edge. The conversation had obviously jolted

Ernie and brought back some deeply-buried memories.

Dr. Harding sat back in his chair and contemplated his answer for a long period of time. Knowing that he had to choose his words wisely. He finally replied, "People respond to extreme tragedy in many different ways, Ernie. Some appear to simply go on with their lives, others suffer years of chronic depression, and still others try to forget by burying themselves in other things, like their work. Personal responses are as varied as the people.

"Let's cut to the chase. We both know that the journal had to have been written by Elizabeth. Even the style in which it was written—not your typical journal at all. The concern I have now is that it is obvious to me that she does not realize that herself. There was no question in my mind when I spoke with her yesterday that Liz was, and is, absolutely convinced the journal was the work of Kathryn, and a troubled Kathryn at that. Therein lies our problem.

"But, that's insane," Ernie shot back. "Liz is Liz. She's completely fine."

"I knew this was going to be tough," Dr. Harding replied. "These things are hard to accept. I'm no psychologist, Ernie, but I truly believe Elizabeth may be suffering a multiple personality disorder brought on by her grief. Some people call it split personality, but that's a real oversimplification. She wrote that journal as someone else, Ernie, and that someone else is convinced she is Kathryn. It's Elizabeth, but it's not Elizabeth, if you understand what I'm saying here."

"That's nothing more than quack science mumbo jumbo," Ernie insisted. "Liz has never shown any signs of that sort of thing, ever, and I would know."

"You think you might, Ernie, but people who are multiple personalities have ways of hiding it. They do have certain controls, in that they know when it's safe for their alternate personality, or personalities, to come out. Each separate personality exerts some level of control over the other, but not always. The symptoms are varied and incredibly complex. That's why it's been so difficult to study or diagnose.

"I know it's hard, Ernie, but at this point I need you to trust me as your doctor, and as your friend."

"I've never had reason not to, Stan, but I must

say that this is pushing it," he replied, a hint of resignation mixed with skepticism showing in his voice.

"Listen," said Dr. Harding. "Elizabeth has given me a few weeks to get back to her on this. I took a little psychology in med. school years ago, but god knows I'm certainly no psychiatrist. A dear friend of mine that I went to school with is, though. Her name is Dr. Claudette Martineau and she's one of Calgary's leading clinical psychiatrists. I would like to run this whole thing past her before we go any further. Are you okay with that?"

Ernie thought for a moment; then nodded without saying a word.

Dr. Harding was not done.

"I know one thing for sure," he said. "Elizabeth is hurting and she has been hurting for quite some time. What's worse is that she's been alone with her pain, unable to share it with anyone. I don't know how it is that I never picked up on it before yesterday when she just pushed it in my face. I'm sure it didn't help her one little bit when I told her those many years ago that she shouldn't have any more children.

"I know you, Ernie," he continued. "I know

you want to go straight home and fix this, but please, whatever you do, don't suddenly start treating her any differently than you have. Believe me when I say that confrontation, in any form, is not going to fix this. She may be more fragile than you and I know. We have to do this together, as a team, and we need real, professional advice before we take one step further.

"I'm going to phone and talk to my psychiatrist friend, Dr. Martineau, tomorrow and I will get back to you, probably very early next week. In the meantime, let's keep this between you and me. I think it's pretty obvious that I never told Elizabeth I was going to talk with you, so me doing so is a big no-no in my business, but I still believe I'm making the right decisions here.

"I have to head out now to visit my hospital patients, Ernie. I would strongly suggest that you stay here and finish reading the journal. I will let Ella know and you can leave when you're done. Just put the journal back in the top right drawer of my desk before you leave."

Ernie left the doctor's office a little under an hour later. His mind was numb, filled with confusion and questions he knew only the future could answer. He wasn't going back to work and it was too early to go home. He decided to do something he had not done for so many years. In fact, he couldn't remember the last time.

He drove his company pick-up truck down to a remote spot by the river just behind an old, temporary mill site his company had abandoned a few years earlier. Ernie remembered coming down here fishing years ago and found it quiet and peaceful; a place where you could close the world out and be with yourself. He shut off the truck's engine, lit a smoke and sat there silently. His thoughts were on Elizabeth, but more, they were on how such a thing as this could have come to pass without him having the slightest clue.

Elizabeth had always been so strong and in raising the family she had shouldered far more than her share. Over the years they had established, almost instinctively and without much discussion, the routines for successfully raising their family. They had brought two very disparate families together and forged them into one; a challenge that had had more than its share of difficult moments.

But the "why" of this whole thing was eluding him. What was it that he wasn't seeing? He loved Elizabeth with all his heart and she him. She had always been a pillar of stability and a woman of exceptional common sense. She had grown up to be that way as one in a large family of dismally poor Saskatchewan dirt farmers, their father a widower before his fortieth birthday. She'd learned early that you bore your burdens quietly and without complaint. You did what you had to do to survive. It left little room for discussion or debate, and certainly not for any self-pity.

Ernie knew he would have to wait for his answers, if they were to come at all. But in his quiet moment there by the river, with still a hundred questions careening around in his head, he made a promise to himself to share the load that Elizabeth had been carrying by herself for so long.

Then he started his truck and drove home for supper; a quiet and lonely affair these days with children no longer there to share the dinner table.

Ernie and Elizabeth spent the warm spring weekend cleaning up the yard in preparation for summer. He welcomed the work and the distractions it provided him from his worries. She seemed her normal self and they worked in silence, each knowing their respective jobs. After all, they'd been tending this yard together for years now and it was their pride and joy.

On Monday morning Ernie got the call at work from Dr. Harding that he had been expecting. Would Tuesday work for him?

"Tuesday's just fine. But," Ernie added, "Can we make it in the morning rather than the afternoon?" He did not want to go through the same torturously anxious day he'd muddled through the previous week.

"Let's make it for 10:30 tomorrow," Dr. Harding suggested. "I'll see you then."

Knowing now what the issues were Ernie was not nearly as distressed as when he'd had that first call from his doctor the previous week. It didn't mean, however, that his concern had abated in the slightest.

He got to Dr. Harding's office just before the appointed time but was alarmed when he noticed his doctor's parking stall was empty. He walked into the waiting room and was relieved at the sight of Ella behind her counter just hanging up the phone.

"Hi Ernie," she greeted him cheerfully. "That was Dr. Harding. He had a bit of an emergency at the hospital this morning, but just called to let me know that he's on his way. Can I get you a coffee while you're waiting?"

"No thanks, Ella," he replied as he slumped into one of the waiting room chairs. "Had one too many this morning already."

Dr. Harding walked through the door ten minutes later, greeted Ella and Ernie in one gesture, then signaled Ernie to follow him into his office. He closed the door behind them and went over and hung his sport jacket on his coat rack. He didn't have to ask Ernie to take a seat. He'd already done so. One of the many things that Ernie liked about his doctor was his complete lack of pretension. He seldom wore a tie, his sport jacket was more for function than form, and Ernie couldn't remember when the sleeves of his dress shirt weren't rolled up.

"I suppose this has been a pretty rough few days for you, Ernie," he said as he sat himself behind his desk.

"Not the best," Ernie replied cryptically.

Getting straight to the point, Dr. Harding continued, "I caught up with my friend, Dr. Martineau this weekend. I called her Friday and we started discussing Elizabeth on the phone. I think I had her totally confused after about half an hour.

"After some time she said to me, 'Listen, Stan, I'm free this weekend. Why don't you just drive up to Calgary and we can get together and discuss this?'

"So that's what I did," Dr. Harding went on. "And I am glad that I did. I hadn't seen Claudette in a long time, so it was a great business/pleasure trip. We discussed everything about Elizabeth's case and she took the time to read the journal cover to cover.

"Incidentally, Ernie, when you read the journal, did you happen to read the short account that was written separately on lined foolscap that was folded and tucked into the front cover pocket; the bit about Ricky's train rescue?"

"Yes, I did," he answered, "And I wondered all weekend why it hadn't been part of the journal itself."

"It's a mystery, for sure. Maybe we'll find out somehow along the way," Dr. Harding replied. "My personal feeling is that Elizabeth wrote that prior to starting the journal, and Dr. Martineau is of the belief that it is what she calls a 'perceptual cue' that led to the writing of the journal."

With that he continued on with his account of

his weekend meeting in Calgary.

"Claudette couldn't resist giving me a strong lecture on the course of action that I've chosen in this matter and she reminded me of the sanctity of doctor/patient confidentiality. By Sunday afternoon, though, she begrudgingly agreed that I had probably done the right thing, given the circumstances."

"You spent two full days with her?" Ernie commented incredulously. "I heard what shrinks get paid these days. This is going to cost a fortune."

"Claudette and I are friends and to be truthful, she became fascinated by Elizabeth's case. This one will be—what is the term that lawyers use? — pro bono.

"Here's the long and short of it, Ernie," Dr. Harding went on. "Dr. Martineau has confirmed my suspicion that Elizabeth is suffering a multiple personality disorder. She's come up short of making this an official diagnosis without actually meeting with Liz herself, so she's cautioned me to consider this only an opinion. She certainly doesn't want to get dragged into an ethical dilemma, and I wouldn't either if I had her six figure practice.

"From her long experience in clinical psychiatry, however, she is certain that this is the result of not one, but two factors. Number one, of course, is the tragedy of her life as you and I talked about last week. Number two is her inability to share her remorse with anyone which is likely due to personality traits ingrained in her from an early age."

"I know she doesn't like worrying me with what she feels are trivialities," Ernie volunteered. "You know how independent she can sometimes seem."

Dr. Harding nodded in agreement.

"She loves you, Ernie. That much is certain. But, she cannot bring herself to burden you with her sadness, so she has done what she has done all her life; she has turned it in on herself, unfortunately, with what appear to be emotionally harmful consequences.

"You two have been an incredible team. I've seen it first hand, as your doctor and your friend. You both understand that you each have your jobs to do and you do them almost instinctively. But I'm willing to bet that somewhere along the way you both got so good at it that you stopped talking to each other.

"I don't mean small, day to day talk, Ernie. I mean talk about each other: how you feel, what troubles you--those sorts of things. I know, it happens to many couples, the difference here being that most of them have not faced the emotional upheavals in their lives that you two have.

"I see it now even in Elizabeth's writings. Here's an issue. Here's how we solve it. Bang! It's fixed. Dr. Martineau caught that one right away. That's just how professional and experienced she is in these matters."

Dr. Harding allowed for a moment of quiet for Ernie to absorb what he had just told him. It wasn't an uncomfortable silence. Ernie was deep in thought.

Finally, he said, "One thing about this whole matter has me truly confounded. The stories in the journal, they're so real, like they actually happened. It's like someone's diary. How could that be?"

"That had me wondering, too," Dr. Harding admitted. "At first."

"Then I realized that Elizabeth is certainly no newcomer to raising children and she grew up in a family with six male siblings. She knows what makes them tick and for sure she knows the full breadth of what they can get up to. She's a voracious reader and she's incredibly intelligent. I don't see it as being any stretch that she is able to write very convincingly. Besides, Ernie, who else do you know who could have possibly written that journal?

"There's a glimmer of good news here, according to Dr. Martineau, but let me go over it carefully with you, Ernie, and listen to me very, very closely, because multiple personality disorder is not something that is easy to wrap your head around. Mental health professionals can no longer deny that it's a real thing, but its symptoms are always a moving target and its diagnosis is never simple.

"Dr. Martineau believes that Elizabeth has not two, but three distinct personas. One is the Elizabeth you know and live with every day. Elizabeth Two is the one who wrote the diary and she may, or perhaps may not, be Kathryn. Dr. Martineau is not quite sure on that one. Elizabeth Three is the one who brought the diary to me last week. She knows nothing of either One or Two, not in the sense that we would understand it, anyway. All three live in the same world, function in the same environment, but for all intents and purposes are oblivious to each other."

"Jekyll and Hyde," Ernie interrupted, almost involuntarily.

"Not exactly the characterization I would use with regard to Elizabeth," Dr. Harding replied, his look unable to cover his slight amusement. "She's anything but dangerous except possibly to herself. But you get the idea. There's nothing new here. I'm sure you've at least heard of the movie The Three Faces of Eve."

Ernie nodded numbly, "That one with Joanne Woodward."

"Yes, well, that's not quite Elizabeth, either, so you can relax a little bit," Dr. Harding continued.

"Dr. Martineau is certain there's a chance for a real positive outcome here. After she'd read the journal she noted something that had completely gone over my head. She asked if I'd realized that the journal's author had, in fact, written herself into a corner, and that the story of Little Ricky appeared to be coming to a close.

"My initial reaction to that, naturally, was one of fear, but she didn't see it that way at all.

"Dr. Martineau believes that by doing what she's done, Elizabeth is calling out for help. She has finally decided that her self-imposed emotional purgatory has to somehow end. If there's a battle going on, Elizabeth One--your Elizabeth, Ernie--may be coming out on top. Dr. Martineau has also suggested that it's highly possible that her visit to my office as Elizabeth Three was yet another tactic in her 'coming out', so to speak—that it was forcing a confrontation.

Another silence fell over the room, broken only by a noisy truck driving past the building.

Ernie was the first to speak.

"So, with all of this professional advice, what do we do now?"

"This is a critical time for Elizabeth, according to Dr. Martineau," Dr. Harding stressed. "How we deal with it can make the difference between her full return to normal or something potentially worse. It is Dr. Martineau's belief, though completely unorthodox, that you, Ernie, are the one person who can best guide her in her recovery, if there is to be a recovery at all."

"Me?" Ernie gasped in shock. "I can barely comprehend what we're even talking about here."

"We're talking about Elizabeth, Ernie. We're talking about making her better. We're talking about a very short window of opportunity. She expects to hear from me in a little over a week from now. I would have nothing to tell her but the truth; that she's ill, which could destroy her right on the spot. The train's left the station on this one. It left the moment I first called you. How we go forth from here may or may not turn out to be the biggest mistake of my life.

"I hate this. I hate where it's gone. I've laid so much on you, Ernie. I feel almost as though I've abandoned my responsibility to Elizabeth and shifted it all onto you, even though you can count on me to be there every step of the way. I'm the doctor. I'm supposed to fix things. But, this isn't a simple attack of appendicitis or a broken leg. I've lain awake every night this week wondering if I've done the right thing. I know that I have, but it still doesn't feel that great.

"Sadly, other than us, there is no help for Elizabeth here. There are no psychiatric facilities nor any qualified mental health experts anywhere within miles. In the meantime, without help, she may be close to a full psychotic break, and could be lost from us for good, though my psychiatrist friend believes the chance of that happening is slim."

There was quiet that followed. Then Ernie responded, "I could not go on without Elizabeth by my side." They were words that Dr. Harding needed to hear; words that told him there was hope here.

"The most critical part will be rebuilding the communication between you and Elizabeth," he explained, casting aside his self-recrimination. "Elizabeth has to know that you are there for her on an emotional level, that you understand that she is in pain.

"It must be gentle and it must be done with the love that only you can give her. Elizabeth has to feel secure and above all, trusting. You must avoid guilt or any threat of confrontation. If you succeed in getting past this, in whatever ways you chose, you will have her back with you, whole, complete and without her demons. And, Ernie, you can't delay. I'm sorry I can't give you more."

There was nothing more to be said. Both Ernie and his doctor stood at once. Dr. Harding came around the big desk and held his friend in a quick embrace, something he hadn't done before but which now seemed appropriate.

"Good luck, my friend," he said. "I want you to know that I will be there for the both of you, as I always have."

Ernie left the office, walked down the short sidewalk, and got back into his truck. He put the keys in the ignition but didn't start it. He sat there for the next five minutes, deep in his own world; a world that in one short week had threatened to totally collapse around him. Then his thoughts turned to Elizabeth, his dear, sweet Liz, and he was hit with the awful realization that her world had been collapsing around her for much, much longer. He hadn't even taken the time to notice.

In spite of what his doctor had cautioned about not delaying, Ernie couldn't just rush home and deal with it. That's not what was meant, he knew, but he also knew that he couldn't sit back and let things run their own course. Through the jumble of psychiatric theory and conjecture everything became simple and crystal clear in Ernie's mind.

Then he made, for him, the oddest of decisions. He was not going to plot this out in his brain like some well-planned business strategy. No, he was simply going to let his heart take over.

Dinner that night was less the solemn affair than it had been so often since the children had all drifted away to make lives of their own. From the moment they had married, both Ernie and Elizabeth had lived with and raised their children, so adjusting their lives to be without them had been difficult.

Thinking back, Liz had realized that they seemed to have lived a life of continual adjustment and that they had been guided by chance rather than the other way around. Both she and Ernie had both been previously married, then each had become single parents, then they married and faced the daunting task of blending their two markedly different families into one. There were social stigmas attached to the circumstances of their early adult lives as well; stigmas that would seem ridiculous just a generation later.

They'd packed the whole tribe up and moved, not just across town to a new neighborhood but to a new community in a new province, to a town that was so culturally removed from what they had become familiar with that it seemed at first like a different country.

This latest adjustment, though--it was turning out to be the toughest. The family banter at the kitchen table, the fights and the ever present need for discipline or mediation were gone now. The common ground upon which Elizabeth and Ernie had built their marriage had slipped away from under them, leaving them with a hollow emptiness that they seemed incapable of sharing. Neither were selfish people, so it had never been in their nature to share any concerns they may have had in this regard for fear it be considered complaining. Both knew, however, that that day would have to come, or they would be sentencing themselves to a life of tedious dreariness.

"Any plans for after supper?" Ernie asked cheerfully, knowing the answer would likely amount to some nondescript solitary task that Elizabeth had set out for herself.

"I was thinking of digging all those stupid perennials out of the flower garden by the garage," she replied. "They're getting out of control."

"Why don't we skip that tonight and I can help you with it another night?" Ernie suggested.

"You got something in mind?" Elizabeth said, a small tone of wariness in her voice.

"Yeah, as a matter of fact, I do," came Ernie's response. "I don't know why, but today I got thinking about the kids and all of the time they spent up Lyons Creek when they were young, talking all the time about Seventeens and Eighteens Falls and a place they all called The Basin. It dawned on me that as long as we've lived here we've never gone up there to see what the big attraction was.

"It's not that far up there, either. Let's take a little hike and see what it's all about."

Elizabeth looked at her husband with skepticism. "Isn't it a bit dangerous hiking up there?" she asked, in what Ernie took to be the weakest of protests.

"The kids said there's a fairly good path right alongside the creek all the way up, and if it gets too difficult we can always just turn around and come home," Ernie coaxed gently, knowing his wife was certainly no mountaineer.

"Well, okay then," she agreed, less reluctantly than Ernie was expecting. "I'll have to dig my sneakers out of the closet, though. I hope they still fit me."

She had a smile on her face, the first real smile that Ernie had seen in a long while. It brought one, involuntarily, to his face as well.

The path wasn't nearly as path-like as the kids had described. Maybe if you were twelve years old and four foot six. Ernie took the lead and was cautious not to let branches swing back and hit his wife in the face. In a few spots the path crossed the creek and followed up the opposite side, only to cross again a few hundred yards further up. Ernie gently took Elizabeth's hand at each crossing and helped her step cautiously from rock to rock. She didn't complain once nor ask to go back. He'd always loved her for her tenacity and pluck.

Just as it seemed they'd gone as far as they dared, they came through a thicket of brush and there it was: a beautiful small pool of water below an eight-foot waterfall that spilled out between two rock outcroppings. Ernie and Elizabeth just stood there, hand in hand, and were speechless. It was gorgeous.

Finally, Ernie turned to Elizabeth and said, "Well, I guess we know now what our kids have been talking about all these years," and without thinking, or questioning even why, he bent to Elizabeth and kissed her tenderly on the lips.

"What was that for?" she said lightly, a smile crossing her face for the second time in less than two hours.

"I don't know," Ernie replied. "Just felt like it."

"Well, if you have to know I kind of liked it," Elizabeth said, her eyes now fixed on the crystal clear pool and the falls that fed it.

"The kids said Eighteens Falls is just a bit further up," Ernie said. "That's where they always went to swim. It's apparently a bit bigger and the pool's deeper than this one."

"I'm a bit bushed," Elizabeth admitted. "Let's save that for another day. This is so pretty here I just want to sit and take it all in. Let's go sit on that dead log over there for a while."

They both sat quietly for a long time and took in all the serenity of their surroundings.

Finally, Ernie said quietly, almost without thought, "I miss the kids." A short pause, then, "I love you." They seemed two separate thoughts, but Elizabeth knew instinctively that they weren't.

She looked up into his face and could see the wet glisten in his eyes.

"Me too," she replied, leaning in and resting her head on his broad shoulder. No more needed to be said.

The hike back to town took less time even though they stopped to pick at a bush of Saskatoon berries they hadn't spotted on the way up. Elizabeth felt somehow lighter on her feet and more agile. She still sought Ernie's help for the occasional creek crossing, but it was more because she knew he wanted to help and she accepted. They arrived back home tired but exhilarated. They hadn't realized how long they'd been gone. The sun was already dipping below the mountain peaks and night was coming on.

Ernie had to go up and check on the lumber drying kiln at the mill. It had been having some difficulties and needed a bit of babysitting. Elizabeth decided to make a pot of tea to be ready when he returned since they'd skipped their usual after supper one. When he returned they had their tea, watched the evening news, prepared the morning coffee and went to bed.

It was a big, double bed, and as was their normal habit they each climbed in on their own side, gave each other a quick good night kiss then assumed the fetal position, back to back. Ernie was restless tonight. It might have been the late night tea. He rolled over onto his back and stared up at the ceiling partially illuminated by the street light outside. He felt no worry and there were no nagging concerns keeping him awake. In fact, he was more at peace than he'd been for quite some time now.

He reached across the bed and touched Elizabeth lightly on the shoulder. She responded to his touch almost immediately, rolled over and moved her body in close to his. She stretched her arm across his middle and rested her head lightly on his chest. They cuddled in silence. A short time later Ernie could tell from her breathing that Elizabeth had drifted off to sleep. He soon followed.

Something had happened since the afternoon. Ernie could feel it. He had wanted to say more to Elizabeth but something told him not to rush. There would be time to talk but not right now.

The next morning, they awoke to find themselves comfortably back to back. Ernie felt the big patch of drool on his pillow and knew he'd slept well.

He slid quietly out of his side of the bed and let Elizabeth sleep. He went out into the kitchen and turned the burner on under the coffee, picked up his Time magazine, lit a cigarette and read until the coffee finished brewing in the big old Pyrex percolator. He didn't absorb much of his magazine this morning. His mind was occupied with other thoughts.

Over his second coffee he opened the can of Vogue tobacco and hand-rolled a dozen more cigarettes for work and placed them in the tin Band-Aid box he'd been using as a cigarette case for years. He noticed he was getting short on wooden matches, so he threw a few more of those in as well. In spite of his job being physically demanding, Ernie had never started his day with breakfast.

Then he went to the basement, put on his work shirt and overalls, grabbed his boots and went back upstairs. Before he put his boots on he went back into the bedroom and gave Liz a soft, good-bye kiss on the cheek. She rustled a bit but didn't wake up. He went back to the porch, put his high top boots on and left for the mill.

Ernie suspected that Liz probably didn't stay in bed long after he left each morning. Starting his noisy work truck, which was always parked right outside their bedroom window would doubtlessly wake her up and the smell of the fresh coffee would draw her into the kitchen. None of this was new. They'd had this routine for years. Even when all the kids were home Ernie had afforded his wife that precious extra fifteen or twenty minutes of morning sleep. To Liz it was a luxury she had accepted without argument.

It was different for her now, though. There were no children left to rustle out of bed in the morning, no listening to the fights over the use of the family's single bathroom, no hasty, last-minute reminders as they went out the back door. There hadn't been that for quite some time. There was no compelling reason for Elizabeth to get out of bed at all, but she did. It was a habit. She poured a cup of coffee for herself, stirred in her Pacific evaporated milk and sat at the kitchen table. Ernie had left his empty coffee cup and magazine there as he always did. Though it annoyed her, deep inside she knew she'd miss it if he were to tidy up after himself.

She sat there, sipped at her hot coffee and gazed out the kitchen window. Elizabeth liked to read, but not in the morning. That was simply not a habit she'd ever gotten into, likely due to the years of morning bedlam she'd endured as a mother. Since the children had all left, she'd occupied herself with writing voluminous letters to her six sisters and a few of her favorite brothers. Their return letters had always been significantly less chatty and a few didn't bother to ever write back at all. In between the letter writing Liz had tried her hand at writing a bit of poetry, but deciding that she was not a poet, after all, they all had ended up crumpled up and stuffed underneath other trash in the garbage can. Bad poetry or not, she did not want Ernie to see it. It would have been embarrassing.

Once again this morning something just seemed amiss as it had every morning since her visit to Dr. Harding's office. She couldn't quite put her finger on it. It was as though it was something that had to be done. What that was exactly was escaping her and it left her with a slight anxiety. But this morning it was far less troubling and persistent than it had been the previous four days. She thought for a long time about the hike up the creek with Ernie the previous evening. It had been unusual, and she had enjoyed every minute of it. The falls had been so lovely her heart had skipped a little when she first saw it. Maybe it was just being out in nature, but the hike had brought her closer to Ernie than she had been in years. She realized just how much she truly loved this man.

Moving to the mountains had not been an easy

transition for her, being a Saskatchewan prairie girl for most of her life. She had lived on the coast, but that hardly resembled the mountain passes of the Rockies, and she had suffered feelings of claustrophobia for the first two or three years. Needless to say, tromping through mountain back country had not been a chosen recreation.

She had a second cup of coffee, this time with some toast and marmalade, did up the dishes and got about her day. There was a bit of ironing to catch up on, then weeding in her garden in the afternoon. She took some leftovers out of the fridge to heat up for Ernie when he got home for lunch. There were always leftovers these days. Elizabeth was still adjusting to cooking for just two people.

Supper that evening was a hasty affair. Wednesdays were Ladies League Night at the golf course and Elizabeth couldn't miss it. This year she was league captain, so it was necessary that she be there. She had her golf in the summer and curling in the winter. She didn't drive, so Ernie chauffeured her to the course and drove back downtown and dropped into the Legion for a couple of cold ones with a few of his cronies that hung out there. There wasn't much to do at home. He drove back to the golf course two hours later and waited until

Elizabeth's foursome came off, then waited while the evening's new standings were posted. They sat around chatting with a group of friends for another half hour then headed home.

Once home, their regular evening routine resumed. Ernie watched a bit of T.V. while Elizabeth busied herself folding a few bed sheets. T.V. was into summer reruns, so Ernie suggested a hand of crib; a game which he felt himself a master at but seldom won, especially against his wife. Elizabeth gave him her standard pre-game warning that if he lost his temper the game would be over—period. As usual, he lost and the game wound up just before the late night news, which they seldom missed. Ernie prepared the coffee for the next morning; then they watched the news and went to bed.

They could have easily slipped back into their old bed habits, but they didn't. Both longed for the intimacy that they had shared the previous evening. Tonight, without prompting, Elizabeth cuddled up close to her husband again and he returned the warmth. They needed no words, but Ernie knew in his heart that certain things could not go unspoken. He feared the fragility of their rediscovered closeness.

Tonight, neither of them fell off to sleep

quickly, and they lay there quietly in each other's arms. It seemed to Ernie as though they were somehow communicating in silence. Words hardly seemed necessary.

The silence of the night was broken by the distant and repeated blasts of the westbound freight train's horn as it approached the town's first crossing. Ernie could feel Elizabeth's body tense, almost imperceptively, at the sound. He said nothing, but brought her even closer.

Then the words came out. The time was right.

"Liz, we have to talk... about our babies."

"Yes," she said.

2:38 P.M. Thursday September 15, 1953
East R.R. Crossing Blairmore

Brenden McLeish fell to his knees at the edge of the track. The train rushed by before him. He didn't feel the hard, sharp crushed rock of the rail bed cutting into his skin. He didn't feel anything.

Tears stung in his eyes as he listened to the screeching steel on steel as the train engineer brought the monster to an emergency stop. His hands covered his eyes, but that didn't erase the image of horror that he had just witnessed.

His heart pounded, almost in time to the relentless clacking of the rail cars as they passed over the crossing.

"If I had run just a little faster I might have saved that poor child? Why did I not see what was happening five seconds earlier?

"Dammit, dammit, dammit. What must have been going through that poor child's mind as that train rushed down on him?

"He saw me coming. I know he saw me coming.
"Maybe his last thought was one of hope.
"Yes, I'm sure it was.

Snatches Blairmore Lad From Path Oncoming Train

WAYNE McALISTER

RICKY GILLIS

Staff Photo: Herald Engraving

COLEMAN — Quick thinking on the part of Wayne McAlister, 19-year-old bridgeman at Blairmore, probably saved the life of five-year-old Ricky Gillis of Blairmore, Saturday morning, when McAlister made a life or death run to snatch from the path of an oncoming CPI Diesel locomotive the youngster standing in the path of the westbound train. Details of the heroic rescue have only now come to light.

According to witnesses the westbound passenger train was proceeding up the track whistling for the crossing at the east end of Blairmore. A number of persons saw a small boy standing on the ties of the railway track, and being too far distant to move the child, called to the boy. McAlister, working on the other side of the now dry creek bed a distance of about 30 yards from where the boy was standing, also saw him. Noticing that the boy was not moving and that the train was very close, Wayne dashed through the river bed and on getting near the boy took what appeared to be a flying jump and snatched the boy out of the way of the train, four feet away from the child.

Although Wayne and the boy fell to the ground, no one suffered injury. Persons who saw the incident say it appeared Ricky was paralyzed with fear as when the train moved near he put his arms up to his eyes and was crying.

Wayne McAlister stated that when he got near the child he heard him say, "It's going to run over me."

To make good his rescue Wayne had to run through a clump of heavy brush, down a steep 30-foot river bank over rocks, then up the steep river bank and for a distance on the flat to get to the boy.

Wayne McAlister, hero of the day, is employed as a bridgeman for the government where he has been working for the past three years. His home is at Claresholm.

Ricky is the son of Mr. and Mrs. Clayton Gillis of Blairmore. Mr. Gillis is employed as a planerman and machinist at the Blairmore sawmills. The Gillis' have three other sons and two daughters at home.

It was learned that Ricky had gone to town with a young friend, Ken Smandych to buy some comic books and had stopped on the tracks to watch the bridgework going on.

Many who saw the thrilling rescue claim that it was "a close shave and had it not been for McAlister's speed and quick thinking a very serious accident, possibly fatal, would have resulted."

BARONS NEWS BRIEFS

BARONS — (HNS) — Mrs. J. Chester, who flew to Vancouver to visit her uncle R. Wiggins, who is sick in hospital, has returned.

Mrs. F. Laurie, who recently underwent an operation in the Galt Hospital, Lethbridge, has returned home.

The Barons carnival will be held Nov. 13 and 14. Games of skill and chance for young and old will be there. The winning queen will be crowned on Saturday evening.

Made in the USA
Charleston, SC
08 February 2017